THE END OF TH

THE HISTORY OF THE LORD OF THE RINGS, PART FOUR

THE HISTORY OF MIDDLE-EARTH

J.R.R. TOLKIEN

THE END OF THE THIRD AGE

The History of
The Lord of the Rings
Part Four

Christopher Tolkien

HOUGHTON MIFFLIN COMPANY
Boston   New York

First Houghton Mifflin paperback edition 2000

Copyright © 1992 by J.R.R. Tolkien Copyright Trust
Foreword, introduction, notes, lists, additional text,
editorial revisions, commentaries, index, and compilation
copyright © 1992, 1998 by Christopher R. Tolkien
Parts of this title were originally published as *Sauron Defeated*.

For information about permission to reproduce selections from
this book, write to Permissions, Houghton Mifflin Company,
215 Park Avenue South, New York, New York 10003.

Visit our Web site: www.hmco.com/trade.

Library of Congress Cataloging-in-Publication Data is available.

ISBN 0-618-08356-1

Printed in the United States of America

QUM 10 9 8 7 6 5 4

CONTENTS

ILLUSTRATIONS

To
TAUM SANTOSKI

EDITOR'S NOTE

As originally published, my history of the writing of *The Lord of the Rings* was not conceived as a separate entity, but formed an integral part of *The History of Middle-earth*; thus Volume 9, entitled *Sauron Defeated*, contains not only the conclusion of the former but also other unconnected works deriving from the same period. These latter are excluded from this edition, and the title of the resulting much shorter book changed to *The End of the Third Age*.

The *Appendices* to *The Lord of the Rings* have been studied in the final volume (12) of the *History*, *The Peoples of Middle-earth* (1996).

There follows here the original Foreword to *Sauron Defeated*, with the omission of some passages that are not relevant to the book in this form.

FOREWORD

With this book my account of the writing of *The Lord of the Rings* is completed. I regret that I did not manage to keep it even within the compass of three fat volumes; but the circumstances were such that it was always difficult to project its structure and foresee its extent, and became more so, since when working on *The Return of the King* I was largely ignorant of what was to come. I shall not attempt a study of the history of the *Appendices* at this time. That work will certainly prove both far-ranging and intricate; and since my father soon turned again, when *The Lord of the Rings* was finished, to the myths and legends of the Elder Days, I hope after this to publish his major writings and rewritings deriving from that period, some of which are wholly unknown.

When *The Lord of the Rings* had still a long way to go – during the halt that lasted through 1945 and extended into 1946, *The Return of the King* being then scarcely begun – my father had embarked on a work of a very different nature: *The Notion Club Papers*; and from this had emerged a new language, Adunaic, and a new and remarkable version of the Númenórean legend, *The Drowning of Anadûnê*, the development of which was closely entwined with that of *The Notion Club Papers*. To retain the chronological order of writing which it has been my aim to follow (so far as I could discover it) in *The History of Middle-earth* I thought at one time to include in Volume VIII, first, the history of the writing of *The Two Towers* (from the point reached in *The Treason of Isengard*) and then this new work of 1945–6, reserving the history of *The Return of the King* to Volume IX. I was persuaded against this, I am sure rightly; and thus it is in the present book that the great disparity of subject-matter appears – and the great difficulty of finding a title for it. My father's suggested title for Book VI of *The Lord of the Rings* was *The End of the Third Age*; but it seemed very unsatisfactory to name this volume *The End of the Third Age and Other Writings*, when the 'other writings', constituting two thirds of the book, were concerned with matters pertaining to the Second Age (and to whatever Age we find ourselves in now).

Sauron Defeated is my best attempt to find some sort of link between the disparate parts and so to name the whole.

I acknowledge with many thanks the help of Dr Judith Priestman of the Bodleian Library, and of Mr Charles B. Elston of Marquette University, in making available photographs for use in this book (from the Bodleian on pages 42 and 138–41, from Marquette those on pages 19 and 130). Mr Charles Noad has again generously given his time to an independent reading of the proofs and checking of citations.

This book is dedicated to Taum Santoski, in gratitude for his support and encouragement throughout my work on *The Lord of the Rings* and in recognition of his long labour in the ordering and preparation for copying of the manuscripts at Marquette, a labour which despite grave and worsening illness he drove himself to complete.

Since this book was set in type Mr Noad has observed and communicated to me the curious fact that in the Plan of Shelob's Lair reproduced in *The War of the Ring*, p. 201, my father's compass-points 'N' and 'S' are reversed. Frodo and Sam were of course moving eastward in the tunnel, and the South was on their right. In my description (p. 200, lines 16 and 20) I evidently followed the compass-points without thinking, and so carelessly wrote of the 'southward' instead of the 'northward' tunnels that left the main tunnel near its eastern end.

THE END OF
THE THIRD AGE

SAURON
DEFEATED

I

THE STORY OF FRODO AND SAM
IN MORDOR

Long foreseen, the story of the destruction of the Ring in the fires of
Mount Doom was slow to reach its final form. I shall look back first
over the earlier conceptions that have appeared in *The Return of the
Shadow* and *The Treason of Isengard*, and then give some further
outlines of the story.

The conception of the Fiery Mountain, in which alone the Ring
could be destroyed, and to which the Quest will ultimately lead, goes
back to the earliest stages in the writing of *The Lord of the Rings*. It
first emerged in Gandalf's conversation with Bingo Bolger-Baggins,
predecessor of Frodo, at Bag End (VI.82): 'I fancy you would have to
find one of the Cracks of Earth in the depths of the Fiery Mountain,
and drop it down into the Secret Fire, if you really wanted to destroy
it.' Already in an outline that almost certainly dates from 1939
(VI.380) the scene on the Mountain appears:

> At end
> When Bingo [> Frodo] at last reaches Crack and Fiery Mountain *he
> cannot make himself throw the Ring away.*   ? He hears Necro-
> mancer's voice offering him great reward – to share power with
> him, if he will keep it.
>   At that moment Gollum – who had seemed to reform and had
> guided them by secret ways through Mordor – comes up and
> treacherously tries to take Ring. They wrestle and Gollum *takes
> Ring* and falls into the Crack.
>   The mountain begins to rumble.

Two years later, in a substantial sketch of the story to come ('The
Story Foreseen from Moria') it was still far from clear to my father just
what happened on the Mountain (VII.209):

> Orodruin [*written above:* Mount Doom] has three great fissures
> North, West, South [> West, South, East] in its sides. They are very
> deep and at an unguessable depth a glow of fire is seen. Every now
> and again fire rolls out of mountain's heart down the terrific
> channels. The mountain towers above Frodo. He comes to a flat
> place on the mountain-side where the fissure is full of fire – Sauron's
> well of fire. The Vultures are coming. He *cannot* throw Ring in. The
> Vultures are coming. All goes dark in his eyes and he falls to his

knees. At that moment Gollum comes up and wrestles with him,
and takes Ring. Frodo falls flat.

Here perhaps Sam comes up, beats off a vulture and hurls himself
and Gollum into the gulf?

Subsequently in this same outline is found:

They escape [from Minas Morgol] but *Gollum follows*.
It is *Sam* that wrestles with Gollum and [?throws] him finally in
the gulf.

Not long after this, in the outline 'The Story Foreseen from Lórien'
(VII.344), my father noted that 'Sam must fall out somehow' (presumably at the beginning of the ascent of Mount Doom) and that Frodo
went up the mountain alone:

Sam must fall out somehow. Stumble and break leg: thinks it is a
crack in ground – really Gollum. [?Makes ?Make] Frodo go on
alone.

Frodo toils up Mount Doom. Earth quakes, the ground is hot.
There is a narrow path winding up. Three fissures. Near summit
there is Sauron's Fire-well. An opening in side of mountain leads
into a chamber the floor of which is split asunder by a cleft.

Frodo turns and looks North-west, sees the dust of battle. Faint
sound of horn. This is Windbeam the Horn of Elendil blown only in
extremity.

Birds circle over. Feet behind.

Since the publication of *The Treason of Isengard* there has come to
light an outline that is obviously closely related to this passage from
'The Story Foreseen from Lórien' (which does not necessarily mean
that it belongs to the same time) but is very much fuller. This I will
refer to as I. The opening sentences were added at the head of the page
but belong with the writing of the text.

(I) Sam falls and hurts leg (really tripped by Gollum). Frodo has to
go alone. (Gollum leaps on Sam as soon as Frodo is away.)

Frodo toils on alone up slope of Mt.Doom. Earth quakes; the
ground becomes hot. There is a narrow path winding up. It crosses
one great fissure by a dreadful bridge. (There are three fissures
(W. S. E.).) Near the summit is 'Sauron's Fire-well'. The path enters
an opening in the side of the Mt. and leads into a low chamber, the
floor of which is split by a profound fissure. Frodo turns back. He
looks NW and sees dust and smoke of battle? (Sound of horn – the
Horn of Elendil?) Suddenly he sees birds circling above: they come
down and he realizes that they are Nazgûl! He crouches in the
chamber-opening but still dare not enter. He hears feet coming up
the path.

At same moment Frodo suddenly feels, many times multiplied, the impact of the (unseen) *searching eye*; and of the enchantment of the Ring. He does not wish to enter chamber or to throw away the Ring. He hears or feels a deep, slow, but urgently persuasive voice speaking: offering him life, peace, honour: rich reward: lordship: power: finally a share in the Great Power – *if* he will stay and go back with a Ring Wraith to Baraddur. This actually terrifies him. He remains immovably balanced between resistance and yielding, tormented, it seems to him a timeless, countless, age. Then suddenly a new thought arose – not from outside – a thought born inside *himself*: *he* would keep the Ring himself, and be master of all. Frodo King of Kings. Hobbits should rule (of course he would not let down his friends) and Frodo rule hobbits. He would make great poems and sing great songs, and all the earth should blossom, and all should be bidden to his feasts. *He puts on the Ring!* A great cry rings out. Nazgûl come swooping down from the North. The *Eye* becomes suddenly like a beam of fire stabbing sheer and sharp out of the northern smoke. He struggles now to take off the Ring – and fails.

The Nazgûl come circling down – ever nearer. With no clear purpose Frodo withdraws into the chamber. Fire boils in the Crack of Doom. All goes dark and Frodo falls to his knees.

At that moment Gollum arrives, panting, and grabs Frodo and the Ring. They fight fiercely on the very brink of the chasm. Gollum breaks Frodo's finger and gets Ring. Frodo falls in a swoon. Sam crawls in while Gollum is dancing in glee and suddenly pushes Gollum into the crack.

Fall of Mordor.

Perhaps better would be to make Gollum repent in a way. He is utterly wretched, and commits suicide. Gollum has it, he cried. No one else shall have it. I will destroy you all. He leaps into crack. Fire goes mad. Frodo is like to be destroyed.

Nazgûl shape at the door. Frodo is caught in the fire-chamber and cannot get out!

Here we all end together, said the Ring Wraith.

Frodo is too weary and lifeless to say nay.

You first, said a voice, and Sam (with Sting?) stabs the Black Rider from behind.

Frodo and Sam escape and flee down mountain-side. But they could not escape the running molten lava. They see Eagles driving the Nazgûl. Eagles rescue them.

Make issue of fire *below* them so that bridge is cut off and *a sea of fire bars their retreat* while mountain quivers and crumbles. Gandalf on *white* eagle rescues them.

Against the sentence 'He is utterly wretched, and commits suicide' my father subsequently wrote *No*.

Another outline, which I will call II, is closely related to outline I just given. It is written in ink over a briefer pencilled text, very little of which can be read – partly because of the overwriting, partly because of the script itself (my father could not read the conclusion of the first sentence and marked it with dots and a query).[1]

(II)   Frodo now feels full force of the Eye .... ? He does not want to enter Chamber of Fire or throw away the Ring. He seems to hear a deep slow persuasive voice speaking: offering life and peace – then rich reward, great wealth – then lordship and power – and finally a share of the Great Power: if he will take Ring intact to the Dark Tower. He rejects this, but stands still – while thought grows (absurd though it may seem): he will keep it, wield it, and himself have Power alone; be Master of All. After all he is a great hero. Hobbits should become lords of men, and he their Lord, King Frodo, Emperor Frodo. He thought of the great poems that would be made, and mighty songs, and saw (as if far away) a great Feast, and himself enthroned and all the kings of the world sitting at his feet, while all the earth blossomed.

(Probably now Sauron is aware of the Ring and its peril, and this is his last desperate throw to halt Frodo, until his messenger can reach Orodruin.)

Frodo puts on Ring! A great cry rings out. A great shadow swoops down from Baraddur, like a bird. The Wizard King is coming. Frodo feels him – the one who stabbed him under Weathertop. He is wearing Ring and has been seen. He struggles to take off Ring and cannot. The Nazgûl draws near as swift as storm. Frodo's one idea is to escape it, and without thinking of his errand he now flies into the Chamber of Fire. A great fissure goes across it from left to right. Fire boils in it. All goes dark to Frodo and he falls on his knees. At that moment *Gollum* arrives panting and grabs at the Ring. That rouses Frodo, and they fight on the brink of the chasm. Gollum breaks Frodo's finger and gets Ring. Frodo falls in swoon. But Sam who has now arrived rushes in suddenly and pushes Gollum over the brink. Gollum and Ring go into the Fire together. The Mountain boils and erupts. Barad-dur falls. A great dust and *a dark shadow* floats away NE on the rising SW wind. Frodo suddenly thinks he can hear and smell Sea. A dreadful shuddering cry is borne away and until it dies far off all men and things stand still.

Frodo turns and sees door blocked by the Wizard King. The mountain begins to erupt and crumble. Here we will perish together, said the Wizard King. But Frodo draws Sting. He no longer has any fear whatsoever. He is master of the Black Riders. He commands the Black Rider to follow the Ring his master and drives it into the Fire.

Then Frodo and Sam fly from the chamber. Fire is pouring out of the mountain-side by three great channels W, SE, S, and makes a burning moat all round. They are cut off.

Gandalf, of course, now knows that Frodo has succeeded and the Ring has perished. He sends Gwaihir the Eagle to see what is happening. Some of the eagles fall withered by flame?[2] But Gwaihir sweeps down and carries off Sam and Frodo back to Gandalf, Aragorn, etc. Joy at the reunion – especially of Merry and Pippin?

There seems to be no certain way in which to date this text, but the reference to the coming of the Wizard King from Barad-dûr shows at any rate that his fate on the Pelennor Fields had not yet arisen. I incline to think that it is relatively late, and would associate it tentatively with the end of the outline 'The Story Foreseen from Forannest' (VIII.362):

Gandalf knows that Ring must have reached fire. Suddenly Sauron is aware of the Ring and its peril. He sees Frodo afar off. In a last desperate attempt he turns his thought from the Battle (so that his men waver again and are pressed back) and tries to stop Frodo. At same time he sends the Wizard King as Nazgûl to the Mountain. The whole plot is clear to him. ...
Gandalf bids Gwaihir fly swiftly to Orodruin.

With this cf. the words of outline II just given: 'Probably now *Sauron is aware of the Ring and its peril*, and this is his *last desperate throw to halt Frodo*'; and 'Gandalf, of course, now knows that Frodo has succeeded and the Ring has perished. He sends Gwaihir the Eagle to see what is happening.'

I turn now to other outlines that preceded any actual narrative writing of Book VI. The first of these, Outline III, also only came to light recently; it is a somewhat disjointed page, with deletions and additions, but all belonging to the same time. I believe that time to be the brief period of work (October 1944) when my father began writing 'Minas Tirith' and 'The Muster of Rohan', and wrote also many outlines for Book V; with the opening of the present text cf. VIII.260: '[12] Gandalf and Aragorn and Éomer and Faramir defeat Mordor. Cross into Ithilien. Ents arrive and Elves out of North. Faramir invests Morghul and main force comes to Morannon. Parley.' It will be seen that the story of the fighting and slaughter in the Tower of Kirith Ungol had not yet arisen.

(III)   They pass into Ithilien [12 >] 11[3] [and turn⌐>] Éomer and Faramir invest Minas Morghul. The rest turn / north to Morannon. Joined by Ents and Elves out of Emyn Muil. Camp on [added: S. edge (of)] Battle Plain [14 >] evening of 12. Parley. Messengers [*sic*] of Sauron. Gandalf refuses. [*Added:* begins assault on Morannon.]

Sam rescues Frodo night of 11/12. They descend into Mordor. [Gollum comes after them. They see a vast host gathering in Kirith Gorgor, and have to lie hid (12). 12/13 They go on and are tracked by Gollum. *This was struck out and replaced by the following:*] Frodo from the high tower holds up phial and as if with Elvish sight[4] sees the white army in Ithilien. On the other side he sees the vast secret host of Mordor (not yet revealed) gathered on the dead fields of Gorgor. ? Sauron delays to take Frodo because of the defeat at Gondor.

Mt.Doom (Orodruin) stands in plain at inner throat of Kirith Gorgor, but a complete darkness comes over land, and all they can see is Mt.Doom's fire and far away the Eye of Baraddur. They cannot find a path? It is not until night of 12 that they reach rocky slopes above the levels of Kirith Gorgor. There they see an immense host camped: it is impossible to go further. They remain in hiding during 13 – and are tracked down by Gollum. Suddenly the whole host strikes camp and pours away leaving Mordor empty. Sauron himself has gone out to war.[5] They cross plain and climb Mt.Doom. Frodo looks back and sees the white army driven back.

Frodo captured on night 10/11. But Shagrat persuades Gorbag not to send message at once,[6] until he's had a look for the *real* warrior still loose. Orcs scatter and hunt in Kirith Ungol (11). Sam at last finds way in – he has to go back and down pass[7] – then he finds quite a small fort[8] of many houses and a gate and a path leading up to the cliff. It is not until [evening >] night of 11 that he manages to get in.

Rescue of Frodo early on 12. Shagrat sends message to Lugburz. [*Added:* How do messages work. Signal from Tower to Eye. News.] Nazgûl arrives at Tower and takes coat of mail and [clothes etc. >] a sword to Baraddur (12).

Frodo and Sam hide in rocks. The Gorgor plain is covered with armies. They are in despair, for crossing is impossible. Slowly they work their way north to where the defile narrows, to a point nearer Mt.Doom [> Dûm].[9]

Another outline (IV) describes the capture of Frodo and his rescue by Sam from the Tower of Kirith Ungol; and this is yet another text of which I was not aware until recently. Like outline II it is written in ink over an underlying, and much briefer, pencilled text. It was written, very obviously at the same time, on the reverse of a page that carries a rejected preliminary version (also in ink over pencil) of the outline 'The march of Aragorn and defeat of the Haradrim' given in VIII.397–9, which preceded the writing of 'The Battle of the Pelennor Fields' and very probably accompanied the outline 'The Story Foreseen from

Forannest' (see VIII.397). This preliminary version of 'The march of Aragorn and defeat of the Haradrim', which contains remarkable features, is given at the end of this chapter (p. 14).

In this outline IV Gorbag is expressly the 'Master of the Tower', whereas in the fair copy manuscript of 'The Choices of Master Samwise' he is the Orc from Minas Morghul, as in RK. It is notable however that at his first appearance in this text he is the Orc from Minas Morghul, changed immediately to Shagrat – which is however marked with a query. This query suggests to me that after so much changing back and forth of the names of these beauties (see VIII.225, note 46) my father could not remember what decision he had come to, and did not at this time check it with the manuscript of the end of Book IV (cf. the case of 'Thror' and 'Thrain', VII.159–60). The same uncertainty is seen in outline III above (see note 6).

(IV)   Frodo is captured night of 10–11. Mar.12 Frodo in prison. (Sauron is distracted by news of the Ents and defeat of his forces in Eastemnet by Ents and Elves of Lórien.)

No message is sent for some time to Dark Tower – partly because of general . . . .[10] Frodo is stripped, and the *Mithril* coat is found.

[Gorbag >] Shagrat (?) covets this, and tries to stop Gorbag sending message: at first pleading need of searching for confederate. But quarrel breaks out, and Shagrat and Gorbag fight and their men take sides. Sam at last finds way in – by a front gate overlooking Mordor – and a steep descent down into a long narrow dale or trough beyond which is a lower ridge.[11] In end Gorbag (Master of the Tower) wins, because he has more men, and Shagrat and all his folk are slain. Gorbag then sends tidings to Baraddur together with the Mithril coat – but overlooks Lórien cloak.[12] Gorbag has only very few men left, and has to send two (since one won't go alone for fear of the missing spy) to Baraddur. Sam slips in and slays one of Gorbag's remaining two at the gate, another on stair, and so wins his way in to the Upper Chamber. There he finds Gorbag. Sam takes off his Ring and fights him and slays him. He then enters Frodo's chamber. Frodo lying bound and naked; he has recovered his wits owing to a draught given him by orcs to counter poison – but he has talked in his delirium and revealed his name and his country, though not his errand.[13] Frodo is filled with fear, for at first he thinks it is an orc that enters. Then hatred for the bearer of the Ring seizes him like a madness, and he reproaches Sam for a traitor and thief. Sam in grief; but he speaks kindly, and the fit passes and Frodo weeps. This is night of 13th. Sam and Frodo escape from Tower on 14th.

It might be a good thing to increase the reckoning of time that Frodo, Sam and Gollum took to climb Kirith Ungol by a day, so that Frodo is not taken until night of 11–12. Quarrel between Orcs on 12th and sending of message that night or morning of 13th when

Gorbag is victorious. Sam gets in on 13th. Otherwise Sam will have to spend all 11, 12 and part of 13 trying to get into Tower.

Make Sam get in before fight and get mixed up with it. And so let Sam hear message sent to Baraddur?

The last outline (V), while written independently of IV, evidently belongs closely with it, and has the same story of the Tower of Kirith Ungol – Gorbag is the captain of the garrison, and Sam slays him. This text, giving the first detailed account of the journey of Frodo and Sam to Mount Doom, is identical in appearance to 'The Story Foreseen from Forannest' and was clearly a companion to it.

At the head of the page are written these notes on distances, which were struck through:

Minas Tirith to Osgiliath (W. end) 24–5 miles. Width of city [*written above:* ruin] 4 miles. East end of Osgiliath to Minas Morghul about 60 miles (52 to Cross Roads?). Minas Morghul to top of Kirith Ungol (and pass below Tower) 15 miles on flat. Kirith Ungol to crest of next (lower) ridge beyond Trough is about 15 miles.

The opening paragraph of the main text is enclosed in square brackets in the original. All the changes shown were made subsequently in pencil, including the reduction of most of the dates by a day.

(V)   [Gorbag sends swift runner to Baraddur on morn(ing) of 13th. He does not reach plain and make contact with any horseman until end [> morn(ing)] of 14th? A rider reaches Baraddur on 15th [> night of 14], and at same time by Nazgûl news of the defeat before Gondor and the coming of Aragorn is brought to him [Sauron].[14] He sends the Nazgûl to Kirith Ungol to learn more. The Nazgûl discovers Tower full of dead and the prisoner flown.]

Sam rescues Frodo and slays Gorbag on 14th [> 13]. Frodo and Sam escape: when clear of the Tower, they disguise themselves in orc-guise. In this way they reach the bottom of the Trough at night on 14th [> 13]. They are surprised that there seems no guard and no one about; but they avoid the road. (A steep stair-path leads down from Tower to join the main road from Minas Morghul over Kirith Ungol pass to the Plain of Mordor and so to Baraddur.) The darkness is that of night.[15]

On 15th [> 14] March they climb the inner ridge – about 1000 feet at most, sheer on W. side, falling in jumbled slopes on E. side. They look out on the Plain of Mordor, but can see little owing to dark [*added:* but the clouds are blown away]. Though by the wizardry of Sauron the air is clear of smokes (so that his troops can move) it hangs like a great pall in the upper air. It seems largely to issue from Orodruin – or so they guess, where far away (50 miles) under the pall there is a great glow, and a gush of flame. Baraddur (further and S. of the Mountain) is mantled in impenetrable shadow. Still, Frodo and Sam can see that all plain is full of troops. Hosts of fires dot the land as far as they can see. They cannot hope to cross. Frodo decides to try and find a point where the open land is narrower, in or nearer to Kirith Gorgor. They descend into Trough again and work north. They begin to count their food anxiously. They are very short of water. Frodo weak after poison – though the orcs gave him something to cure it, and *lembas* seems specially good as antidote; he cannot go fast.[16] They manage 10 miles along Trough.

On 16th [> 15] they continue to crawl along Trough, until they are some 25–30 miles north of Kirith Ungol.

On 17th [> 16] they climb ridge again, and lie hid. They hardly dare move again even in the gloom, since they can see below them great hosts of warriors marching into the defile out of Mordor. Frodo guesses they are going to war and wonders what is happening to Gandalf etc. [*Added:* No, most of troops are now *coming back in*.]

On 19th [> 18] being desperate they go down and hide in the rocks at the edge of the defile. At last Sauron's troop-movements cease. There is an ominous silence. Sauron is waiting for Gandalf to come into trap. Night of 19–20 [> 18–19] Frodo and Sam try to cross the defile into Ered-Lithui. (About this time let Sam have suspicion that Gollum is still about, but say nothing to Frodo?)

After various adventures they get to Eredlithui at a point about 55 miles NW of Orodruin. 20 (part), 21, 22, 23 they are working along slopes of Eredlithui.[17]

On 24th their food and water is all spent – and Frodo has little strength left. Sam feels a blindness coming on and wonders if it is due to water of Mordor.

24th. Frodo with a last effort – too desperate for fear – reaches foot of Orodruin and on 25 begins the ascent. There is a constant rumble underground like a war of thunder. It is night. Frodo looks round fearing the ascent – a great compulsion of reluctance is on him. He feels the weight of the Eye. And behold the mantle of shadow over Baraddur is drawn aside: and like a window looking into an inner fire he sees the Eye. He falls in a faint – but the regard of the Eye is really towards Kirith Gorgor and the coming battle, and it sweeps past Orodruin.

Frodo recovers and begins ascent of Mt.Doom. He finds a winding path that leads up to some unknown destination; but it is cut across by wide fissures. The whole mountain is shaking. Sam half-blind is lagging behind. He trips and falls – but calls to Frodo to go on: and then suddenly Gollum has him from behind and chokes his cries. Frodo goes on alone not knowing that Sam is not behind, and is in danger. Gollum would have killed Sam but is suddenly filled with fear lest Frodo destroy Ring. Sam is half throttled, but he struggles on as soon as Gollum releases him.

Here the text ends, and at the end my father wrote in pencil: 'Carry on now with old sketch.' Possibly he was referring to outline II (p. 6), although there seems reason to think (p. 7) that that outline belongs to much the same time as the present text.

★

The chronology of writing

I take it as certain that my father took up *The Lord of the Rings* again, after the long halt at the end of 1944, in the latter part of 1946: this was when he returned to the abandoned openings of the chapters 'Minas Tirith' and 'The Muster of Rohan'. For the subsequent chronology of writing there is little evidence beyond the rather obscure statements in his letters. On 30 September 1946 (*Letters* no.106, to Stanley Unwin) he said that he 'picked it up again last week' and wrote a further chapter, but there is really no knowing what this was; and on 7 December 1946 (*Letters* no.107, to Stanley Unwin) he wrote: 'I still hope shortly to finish my "magnum opus": the Lord of the Rings: and let you see it, before long, or before January. I am on the last chapters.'

In an unpublished letter to Stanley Unwin of 5 May 1947 he wrote: 'It [Farmer Giles] is hardly a worthy successor to "The Hobbit", but on the real sequel life hardly allows me any time to work'; and in another of 28 May 'I have not had a chance to do any writing.' On 31 July 1947 (*Letters* no.109) he was saying: 'The thing is to finish the thing as devised and then let it be judged'; and a further eight months on (7 April 1948, *Letters* no.114, to Hugh Brogan) he wrote: 'Only the difficulty of writing the last chapters, and the shortage of paper have so far prevented its printing. I hope at least to finish it this year ...' Then, on 31 October 1948 (*Letters* no.117, again to Hugh Brogan), he said, 'I managed to go into "retreat" in the summer, and am happy to announce that I succeeded at last in bringing the "Lord of the Rings" to a successful conclusion.'

The only other evidence that I know of is found in two pages on which my father made a list of candidates for an academic post with notes on their previous experience. Against several of the names he noted both date of birth and present age, from which it is clear that the year was 1948. On the reverse of one of these pages is drafting for the passage in 'The Land of Shadow' in which Frodo and Sam see the darkness of Mordor being driven back (RK p. 196); the second part is overwritten with drafting for the discussion of food and water in 'The Tower of Kirith Ungol' (RK p. 190), while the reverse of it carries very rough sketching of the discovery of Frodo by Sam in the Tower.

Thus in December 1946 he was 'on the last chapters' of *The Lord of the Rings*, and hoped to finish it 'before January'; but in 1948 he was drafting the opening chapters of Book VI. The explanation must be, I think, that by the end of 1946 he had completed or largely completed Book V, and so (in relation to the whole work) he could feel that he was now 'on the last chapters'; and greatly underestimating (as he had so often done before) how much needed to be told before he reached the end, he thought that he could finish it within the month. But 1947 was largely unproductive, as the letters imply; and Book VI was not written until 1948.

NOTES

1 The few words and sentences that I can make out are sufficient to show that the story in the underlying text was substantially the same. The ink overwriting ends before the pencilled text does, and the last sentence of the latter can be read: 'Thorndor sweeps down and carries off Sam and Frodo. They rejoin the host on Battle Plain.' The naming of the rescuing eagle *Thorndor* (earlier form of *Thorondor*) is very surprising, but is perhaps to be explained as an unconscious reminiscence (when writing at great speed) of the rescue of Beren and Lúthien in *The Silmarillion*.

2 Cf. the fate of the Nazgûl in RK (p. 224): 'And into the heart of the storm ... the Nazgûl came, shooting like flaming bolts, as caught in the fiery ruin of hill and sky they crackled, withered, and went out.'

3 The dates are still in February. For the change in the month see VIII.324–5; and with the chronology of this text cf. that given in VIII.226.

4 Cf. the outline 'The Story Foreseen from Fangorn' (VII.438): 'Then return to Frodo. Make him look out onto impenetrable night. Then use phial which has escaped ... By its light he sees the forces of deliverance approach and the dark host go out to meet them.' On this I remarked (VII.440, note 15): 'The light of the Phial of Galadriel must be conceived here to be of huge power, a veritable star in the darkness.'

5 *Sauron himself has gone out to war*: despite the apparent plain significance of the words, it is impossible that my father should have meant that Sauron was no longer present in the Dark Tower.

6 *Gorbag* replaced *Yagûl* as the name of the Orc from Minas Morghul in the fair copy manuscript of 'The Choices of Master Samwise' (see VIII.225, note 46). Here 'Shagrat persuades Gorbag not to send message at once' suggests that Gorbag is the Orc from the Tower, whereas a few lines later 'Shagrat sends message to Lugburz'; see further outline IV, p. 9.

7   *he has to go back and down pass:* i.e., Sam had to go back out of
     the tunnels and up to the pass, then down the other side of it (cf.
     RK pp. 173–5).
8   *quite a small fort:* I think that this means, not 'only a *small* fort',
     but 'an actual fort, if not very large, not simply a tower'.
9   For the spelling *Mount Dûm* see VII.373, VIII.118.
10   My father could not read the pencilled words here and wrote
     queries against them.
11   This is the first description of the Morgai (which is marked and
     named on the Second Map, VIII.435, 438).
12   The outline 'The march of Aragorn and defeat of the Haradrim',
     closely associated with the present text, has a brief passage about
     the rescue of Frodo concerned with the cloak of Lórien
     (VIII.398):
        Rescue of Frodo. Frodo is lying naked in the Tower; but Sam
        finds by some chance that the elven-cloak of Lórien is lying in a
        corner. When they disguise themselves they put on the grey
        cloaks over all and become practically invisible – in Mordor the
        cloaks of the Elves become like a dark mantle of shadow.
13   Cf. 'The Story Foreseen from Forannest' (VIII.361):
        He [the ambassador of Sauron to the Parley] bears the Mithril
        coat and says that Sauron has already captured the messenger –
        a *hobbit*. How does Sauron know? He would of course guess
        from Gollum's previous visits that a small messenger might be
        a *hobbit*. But it is probable that either Frodo *talked in his
        drugged sleep* – not of the Ring, but of his name and country;
        and that Gorbag had sent tidings.
14   A pencilled X is written against this sentence. Cf. 'The Story
     Foreseen from Forannest' (VIII.360): 'Sauron ... first hears of
     Frodo on 15 of March, and at the same time, by Nazgûl, of the
     defeat in Pelennor and the coming of Aragorn. ... He sends the
     Nazgûl to Kirith Ungol to get Frodo ...'
15   Against this paragraph is written in the margin: 'Frodo's horror
     when Sam comes in and looks like a goblin. Hate for the
     Ringbearer seizes him and bitter words of reproach for treachery
     spring to his lips.'
16   In the margin is written here: 'Ring a great burden, worse since he
     had been for a while free of it.'
17   Beside these dates is written '10 miles, 15, 15, 15'.

★

*The rejected preliminary version of 'The March of Aragorn
and defeat of the Haradrim'*

I have mentioned (pp. 8–9) that on the reverse of the page bearing
outline IV (describing the capture and rescue of Frodo) is the original

form of the outline given in VIII.397–9, entitled 'The march of Aragorn and defeat of the Haradrim'. This is a very puzzling text, and I give it in full. It was in fact written in three forms. The first is a pencilled text (a) as follows:

Aragorn takes Paths of the Dead early on March 8th. Comes out of the tunnel (a grievous road) and reaches head of the Vale of Morthond at dusk. He blows horns [*struck out:* and unfurls standard] to amazement of the people; who acclaim [him] as a king risen from the Dead. He rests three hours and bidding all to follow and send out the war-arrows he rides for the Stone of Erech. This is a stone set up between the mouths of Lamedui and the Ethir Anduin delta to commemorate the landing of Isildur and Anárion. It is about 275 miles by road from the issuing of the Paths of the Dead. Aragorn rides 100 miles and reaches the Ringlo Vale (where men are assembling) on March 9. There he gathers news and men. He rides after short rest into Lamedon (10) and then goes to

Here this version was abandoned and a new start made, also in pencil, at 'Aragorn takes Paths of the Dead'; but this text (b) was overwritten in ink and can only be read here and there. The overwritten form (c) reads thus:

Aragorn takes Paths of the Dead morn(ing) 8 March, passes tunnels of the mountains and comes out into the head of Morthond Vale at dusk. Men of the Dale are filled with fear for it seems to them that behind the dark shapes of the living riders a great host of shadowy men come nearly as swift as riders. Aragorn goes on through night and reaches Stone of Erech at morn(ing) on March 9. Stone of Erech was black stone fabled to have been brought from Númenor, and set to mark the landing of Isildur and Anárion and their reception as kings by the dark men of the land. It stood on the shores of Cobas, near the outflow of Morthond, and about it was a ruined wall within which was also a ruined tower. In the vault under the tower forgotten was one of the Palantir[i]. From Erech a road ran by [the] sea, skirting in a loop the hills of Tarnost, and so to Ethir Anduin and the Lebennin.

At Stone of Erech Aragorn unfurls his standard (Isildur's) with white crown and star and Tree and blows horns. Men come to him. (The Shadow-men cannot be seen by day.) Aragorn learns that what he saw in Palantir was true indeed: Men of Harad have landed on the coasts near the Ethir, and their ships have sailed up the estuary as far as Pelargir. There the men of Lebennin have made a block – on the basis of an ancient defence. The Haradwaith are ravaging the land. It is nearly 350 miles by coast road from Erech to Pelargir. Aragorn sends out swift riders north into the Dales, summoning what men remain to march on Pelargir. He does not himself take

coast-road, since it is infested, but after a rest he sets out at dusk of
March 9 – and goes like wind by rough paths over Linhir and so to
Fords of Lameduin (about 150 miles away). The Shadow Host is
seen to follow. He crosses Morthond at Linhir, passes into Ringlo
Vale, and sets all land aflame for war. He reaches Lameduin evening
of March 10. Men are assembled there, and are resisting an attempt
of the Haradwaith to cross Lebennin > NW. Aragorn and the
Shadow Host come out of the dark with the white star shining on
the banner and the Haradwaith are terrified. Many drowned in the
river Lameduin. Aragorn camps and crosses Lameduin into Lebennin and marches on Pelargir morn(ing) of 11 March. The terror of
'the Black King' precedes him, and the Haradwaith try to fly: some
ships escape down Anduin, but Aragorn comes up driving Haradwaith before him. The Shadow Host camps on shores of Anduin
before Pelargir on evening of March 11th. By night they set fire in
guarded ships, destroy the Haradwaith and capture 2 vessels. On
morn(ing) of 12th they set out up Anduin, with Haradwaith
captains rowing.

The extraordinary thing about this, of course, is the site of Erech. It
seems plain beyond any question from all the evidence presented in
The War of the Ring (see especially the chapter 'Many Roads Lead
Eastward (1)') that from its first emergence Erech was in the southern
foothills of Ered Nimrais, near the source of Morthond: Erech stands
self-evidently in close relationship with the Paths of the Dead. Why
then did my father now move it, first (in a) to the coast between the
mouths of Lameduin and Ethir Anduin, and then (in b and c) to Cobas
Haven (north of Dol Amroth: see the Second Map, VIII.434)? I am
unable to propose any explanation.

The geography of the c-version is at first sight hard to follow. In a
Aragorn's route can be understood: all that is said here is that he rode
from the head of Morthond Vale 'for the Stone of Erech'; he reaches
the Ringlo Vale, and then continues into Lamedon (which at this stage
lay east of the river Lameduin: see VIII.437). The distance of 275 miles
from the issuing of the Paths of the Dead to Erech 'between the
mouths of Lamedui and the Ethir Anduin delta' is however much too
great, and was perhaps an error for 175. (On the form Lamedui see
VIII.436.) In version c, however, Aragorn leaves Erech 'on the shores
of Cobas, near the outflow of Morthond', and 'goes like wind by
rough paths over Linhir and so to Fords of Lameduin (about 150
miles away). ... He crosses Morthond at Linhir, passes into Ringlo
Vale ... He reaches Lameduin.' As it stands this makes no sense; but
the explanation is that his journey is described twice in the same
passage. The first statement is comprised in the words 'He goes like
wind by rough paths over Linhir, and so to Fords of Lameduin (about
150 miles away).' The second statement is 'He crosses Morthond at

Linhir, passes into Ringlo Vale ... He reaches Lameduin.' This must mean that Linhir is here in the earlier position, above Cobas Haven (see VIII.437).

It is said in c that the coast road from Erech skirted in a loop 'the Hills of Tarnost'. This name is written in pencil against a dot on the square Q 12 of the Second Map, at the northern extremity of the hills between the rivers Lameduin and Ringlo (see VIII.434, 437, where I said that so far as I then knew the name *Tarnost* does not occur elsewhere).

Lastly, in the concluding lines of b, which were not overwritten, the name *Haradrians* is given to the Haradwaith.

II

THE TOWER OF KIRITH UNGOL

It seems that my father returned to the story of Frodo and Sam more than three years after he had 'got the hero into such a fix' (as he said in a letter of November 1944, VIII.218) 'that not even an author will be able to extricate him without labour and difficulty.' As one of the outlines given in the preceding chapter shows, however, he had continued to give thought to the question, and while Book V was still in progress he had discovered the essential element in Sam's rescue of Frodo: the quarrel of Shagrat and Gorbag in the Tower of Kirith Ungol, leading to the mutual slaughter of almost all the orcs both of the Tower and of Minas Morgul before Sam arrived (p. 9).

His first draft ('A') of the new chapter extended as far as the point where Sam, descending the path from the Cleft, sees the two orcs shot down as they ran from the gateway of the Tower, and looking up at the masonry of the walls on his left realises that to enter in 'the gate was the only way' (RK p. 178). In this draft the text of RK was largely achieved, but not in all respects. In the first place, the chapter begins thus: 'For a while Sam stood stunned before the closed door. Far within he heard the sounds of orc-voices clamouring...' It is clear that he was not physically stunned, as he was in the final story. On this see pp. 21–2.[1]

Secondly, when Sam, groping his way back from the under-gate in the tunnel, wondered about his friends (RK p. 173), 'Out in the world it was the dark before dawn on the twelfth of March in Shire-reckoning, the third day since he and Frodo came to the Cross Roads, and Aragorn was drawing near to Anduin and the fleet of Umbar, and Merry was beginning the third day of his ride from Dunharrow, and the forest of Druadan lay before him; but in Minas Tirith Pippin stood sleepless on the walls [?waiting] for [the] Causeway Forts had fallen and the enemy was coming.'

Thirdly, the fortress of Kirith Ungol was at first conceived as rising 'in four great tiers', not three as in RK (p. 176), and its strange structure, as it were flowing down the mountain-side, is sketched on the page of the draft (reproduced on p. 19) beside the description in the text; this description, originally in pencil but overwritten in ink, runs as follows:

And in that dreadful light Sam stood aghast; for now he could see the Tower of Kirith Ungol in all its strength. The horn that

The Tower of Kirith Ungol

those could see who came up the pass from the West was but its topmost turret. Its eastern face stood up in four great tiers from a shelf in the mountain wall some 500 feet below. Its back was to the great cliff behind, and it was built in four pointed bastions of cunning masonry, with sides facing north-east and south-east, one above the other, diminishing* as they went up, while about the lowest tier was a battlemented wall enclosing a narrow courtyard. Its gate open[ed] on the SE into a broad road. The wall at the [?outward] .... was upon the brink of a precipice.

   *[The bottom one was probably projected some 50 yards from the cliff, the next 40, the next 30, the top 20 – and on the top [or tip] of it was the turret-tower. Their heights were 50 ft., 40 ft., 30 ft., 20 ?]

With black blank eyes the windows stared over the plains of Gorgoroth and Lithlad; some [?form(ed)] a line of red-lit holes, climbing up. Maybe they marked some stair up to the turret.

   With a sudden shock of perception Sam realized that this stronghold had been built not to keep people out of Mordor, but to keep them in! It was indeed in origin one of the works of Gondor long ago: the easternmost outpost of the defence of Ithilien and Minas Ithil, made when after the overthrow of Sauron, in the days of the Last Alliance, the Men of the West kept watch upon the evil land where still his creatures lurked. But as with the Towers of the Teeth that watch[ed] over Kirith Gorgor, Nargos and ? [sic][2], so here too the watch and ward had failed and treachery had yielded up the Tower to the Ringwraiths. [?And] now for long it had been occupied by evil things. And since his return to Mordor Sauron had found it useful.

   The pencilled passage that follows the end of the overwriting in ink reads as follows:

... keep watch upon the evil land where still his creatures lurked. But as with the Towers of the Teeth upon Kirith Gorgor, so here the watch and ward had failed and treachery had yielded up the Tower. But Sauron too had found it useful. For he had few servants and many slaves. Still its purpose was as of old to keep people in.

   Sam looked and he saw how the tower commanded the main road from the pass behind; the road he was on was only a narrow way that went corkscrewing down into the darkness and seemed to join a broad way from the gate to the road.

This page was removed from the original draft text A on account of the illustration (the only one that my father ever made of the Tower of Kirith Ungol), which was squared off with rough lines, and placed with the second fair copy manuscript (E), although by then the fortress was built in three tiers not four.

This original draft continues on to its end thus, and in this appears the most important difference from the story of RK (pp. 176–8):

There was no doubt of the path he must take, but the longer he looked the less he liked it. He put on the Ring again and began to go down. Now he could hear the cries and sounds of fighting again. He was about halfway down when out of the dark gate into the red glow came two orcs running. They did not turn his way but were making for the main road, when they fell and lay still. Apparently they had been shot down by others from the wall of the lower course or from the shadow of the gate.[3] After that no more came out. Sam went on. He came now [to] the point where [the] descending path hugged the lower wall of the tower as it stood out from the rock behind. There was a narrow angle there. He stopped again, glad of the excuse; but he soon saw that there was no way in. There was no purchase in the smooth rock or [?jointed] masonry and 100 feet above the wall hung beetling out. The gate was the only way.

Here the first draft stops. Thus the entire passage in RK (p. 177) in which Sam is tempted to put on the Ring and claim it for his own, his mind filling with grandiose fantasies (deriving from those of Frodo on Mount Doom in outlines I and II, pp. 5–6), is lacking; but at the point where the draft ends my father wrote (clearly at the same time): *Sam must not wear Ring.* No doubt it was this perception that caused him to abandon this text.

He began at once on a second draft, 'B', for most of its length written legibly in ink, with the number 'LII'[4] and the title 'The Tower of Kirith Ungol'. This opened in the same way as did A (p. 18): 'For a while Sam stood stunned before the closed door. Far within he heard the sounds of orc-voices clamouring . . .' In the fair copy manuscript of 'The Choices of Master Samwise' it had been said (following the original draft) that 'Sam hurled himself against it, and fell', changed in pencil to 'Sam hurled himself against the bolted plates, and fell to the ground.' This was repeated in the first typescript of that chapter; only in the second typescript was the word 'senseless' introduced. The explanation of this is that while writing the present draft B of 'The Tower of Kirith Ungol' my father was struck by a thought which he noted in the margin of the page, telling himself that he 'must leave time for Frodo to recover and to fight'[5] and that in order to achieve this

'Sam must *swoon* outside the undergate.' It was no doubt at this time
that he changed the opening of B:

> For a while Sam stood dumb before the closed door. Then desperate
> and mad he charged at the brazen door, and fell back stunned;
> down into darkness he sank. How long it lasted he could not tell;
> but when he came to himself still all was dark.

Against the passage in the draft A referring to other events in the
world at that hour (p. 18) my father noted: 'Make Frodo and Sam one
day more in Epheldúath. So Frodo is captured night of 12, when
Merry was in Druadan Forest and Faramir lay in fever and Pippin was
with the Lord, but Aragorn was manning his fleet.' In B the passage
now becomes:

> Out westward in the world it was deep night upon the twelfth of
> March by Shire-reckoning, three days since he and Frodo had
> passed the peril of Minas Morgul; and now Aragorn was manning
> the black fleet on Anduin, and Merry in the Forest of Druadan was
> listening to the Wild Man, while in Minas Tirith the flames were
> roaring and [the great assault upon the Gates had begun >] the
> Lord sat beside the bed of Faramir in the White Tower.

Against 'March' in this passage my father scribbled in the margin:
'Make Hobbit names of months.'

At the point where Sam at the crest of the pass looked out over
Mordor to Orodruin ('the light of it ... now glared against the stark
rock faces, so that they seemed to be drenched with blood', RK p. 176)
my father halted briefly and wrote the following note across the page:

> Change in the Ring as it comes in sight of the furnace where it was
> made. Sam feels *large* – and naked. He knows that he must *not* use
> the Ring or challenge the Eye; and he knows he is not big enough for
> that. The Ring is to be a desperate burden and no help from now
> onwards.

The Tower of Kirith Ungol is still built in four tiers, not three, and
the note concerning the dimensions of the bastions was retained (see
p. 20), though the dimensions were changed:

> [The bottom tier projected some 40 yards from the nearly perpen-
> dicular cliff, the second 30, the third 20, the topmost 10; and their
> height diminished similarly, 80 ft., 70 ft., 60 ft., 40 ft., and the
> topmost turret some 50 ft. above the top of .... mountain wall.]

The road from Minas Morgul over the Pass of Morgul is said here to
pass 'through a jagged cleft in the inner ridge out into the valley of
Gorgor on its way to the Dark Tower'; the name *Morgai* had not yet
been devised (cf. RK p. 176). *Gorgor* was changed, probably im-

mediately, to *Gorgoroth* (cf. VIII.256). The Towers of the Teeth were at first not named in this text, but *Narchost and Carchost* was added in subsequently.

Following the note on the subject of the Ring just given, this draft now effectively reaches the text of RK in the account of Sam's temptation and his refusal of it, as far as the point where A ended ('The gate was the only way', RK p. 178). From this point B becomes rough and is partly in outline form.

Sam wonders how many orcs lived in the Tower with Shagrat and how many men Gorbag had [*marginal note:* Make Gorbag's men more numerous in last chapter of Book IV][6] and what all the fighting was about. 'Now for it!' he cried. He drew Sting and ran towards the open gate – only to feel a shock, as if he had run into some web like Shelob's but *invisible*. He could see no obstacle, but something too strong for his will to overcome barred the way. Then just inside the gate he saw the Two Watchers. They were as far as he could see in the gloom like great figures sitting on chairs, each had three bodies, and three heads, and their legs facing inward and outward and across the gateway. Their heads were like vulture-faces, and on their knees were laid clawlike hands.[7] They were carved of black stone, it seemed, moveless, and yet they were aware; some dreadful spirit of evil vigilance dwelt in them. They knew an enemy, and forbade his entry (or escape). Greatly daring, because there was now nothing else to do, Sam drew out the phial of Galadriel. He seemed to see a glitter in the jet-wrought eyes of the Watchers, but slowly he felt their opposition melt into fear. He sprang through, but even as he did so, as if it was some signal given by the Watchers, far up in the Tower he heard a shrill cry.

In RK (p. 179), even as Sam sprang through the gateway, 'he was aware, as plainly as if a bar of steel had snapped to behind him, that their vigilance was renewed. And from those evil heads there came a high shrill cry that echoed in the towering walls before him. Far up above, like an answering signal, a harsh bell clanged a single stroke.' In the margin of the present text, against the foregoing passage, is a note: 'Or make Watchers close with a snap. Sam is in a trap once more.'

The courtyard was full of slain orcs. Some lay here and there, hewn down or shot, but many lay still grappling one another, as they throttled or stabbed their opponents. Two archers right in the gateway – probably those who shot down the escaping orcs – lay pierced from behind with spears. [Sting, Sam noticed, was only shining faintly.]

Sam rushed across the court, and to his relief found the door at the base of the Tower ajar. He met no one. Torches are flaring in brackets. A stair, opening on right, goes up. He runs up it, and so out into the narrow yard before the second door. 'Well!' he said to himself, his spirits rising a little, 'Well! It looks as if Shagrat or Gorbag was on my side and has done my job for me. There's nobody left alive!' And with that he halted, suddenly realizing the full meaning of what he had said: nobody was left alive. 'Frodo! Frodo!' he called, forgetful of all else, and ran to the second door. An orc leaps out at him [*in margin:* Two orcs].

Sam kills the [> one] orc and the other runs off yelling for Shagrat. Sam climbs warily. The stair now rises at the back of the entrance passage, and climbs right up to the Turret (the Brazen Gate enters about on a level with the courtyard?). Sam hears voices, and stalks them. The orc is pattering away up the stairs. 'Shagrat!' he calls. 'Here he is, the other spy.' Sam follows. He overhears the orc reporting to Shagrat. Shagrat is lying wounded by dead body of Gorbag. All Gorbag's men have been killed, but they have killed all Shagrat's but these two.

An isolated slip of paper seems very likely to be the continuation of this outline, and the first sketching of the new story of the escape from the Tower. The writing declines towards the end into such a scrawl that many words and phrases are impossible to make out.

Shagrat has in vain tried to get messages away to Baraddûr. The Quarrel arose about the treasures. Gorbag coveted the mithril coat, but pretended that they must search for the missing spy first. He sent his men to capture wall and gate, and demanded mithril coat. But Shagrat won't agree. Frodo was thrust in chamber of turret and stripped. Shagrat gives him some medicine and begins to question him. Shagrat puts things together to send to Baraddur (Lugburz). Gorbag tries to fight way in and slay Frodo.

Gorbag and Shagrat fight.

When Shagrat hears news (although orc says the other spy is not a large warrior) he is frightened, as he is wounded. He makes the treasures into a bundle and tries to creep off. He must get to Lugburz. So when Sam leaps out with phial and shining sword he flees. Sam pursues; but gives up for he [?hears] Frodo

[?crying]. He sees Shagrat far below rushing out of gate – and does not at first realize the misfortune of news getting to Lugburz. The orc left behind is tormenting Frodo. Sam rushes in and slays him.

Scene of yielding up Ring. Frodo has lost his cloak and ....[8] He has to dress in the orc's clothes [*or* in orcs' clothes]. Sam does likewise but keeps cloak and Sting. Frodo has to have orc-weapons. The sword is gone.[9] He tells Sam about the fight. They make their plans.

The opposition of the Watchers. The Tower seems full of evil. Cry goes up as they escape. And as if in answer a Nazgûl comes dropping down out of the black sky, [?shining .... ?with] a fell red, and perches on the wall. Meanwhile they dash down the road, and as soon as they can leave it and climb into the shelter of the rocks near bottom of trough. They wonder what to do.

Food.[10] Drink. They had found Frodo's sack and ..... [?in corner] rummaged – but orcs would not touch *lembas*. They gathered up what was left of it, in broken fragments. Orcs must drink. [?They see] [a] well in the courtyard. Sam tastes it – says Frodo not to risk it. It seems all right. They fill their water bottles. It is now 13th of March, make it 14th? They reckoned they have [?enough] for about a week with care or at a desperate pinch ten days. How far is it.

They climb to lower ridge and find they dare not go across the plain at that point – where it is broad and full of enemies.

The Nazgûl [?explores] Tower and sees there is [??trouble] and flies off. Frodo thinks it best to go north to where the plain narrows – he had seen sketch of Mordor in Elrond's house – and away from Kirith Ungol to which [??attention is now directed]. He bemoans fact that Shagrat had got away with *tokens*.

Chapter ends with the Nazgûl shining red circling over Tower [??and he cries as] ..... of orcs begin to search the [?pass] and the road and lands about.

I believe that at this stage my father began the chapter again, and this was the first completed manuscript ('D'). It was numbered 'LII' but given a new title 'The Orc-tower'; the number was later changed to 'L' (which I cannot explain) and the title 'The Tower of Kirith Ungol' (which it had borne in the draft B) restored.

New initial drafting begins at the point where Sam enters the gate of the Tower, but up to this point the final text was now written out on the basis of the drafts A and B described above, in a form only differing in a few minor points from that in RK. The chapter now opens exactly as it does in the published work (see p. 22), and Sam now has to climb back over the stone door leading into the passage to the under-gate, since he still cannot find the catch (note 1). The events 'out westward in the world' are described in the same words as in RK (with the addition, after 'Pippin watched the madness growing in the eyes of Denethor', of 'and Gandalf laboured in the last defence'); but the date ('noon upon the fourteenth day of March' in RK) is now 'morning upon the thirteenth day of March'. The name *Morgai* appears as an early addition to the text (p. 22). The Tower now has three tiers, and the note about the dimensions of the bastions, still present (see pp. 20, 22), was accommodated to this: the tiers now projected 40, 30 and 20 yards from the cliff, and their heights were 80, 70, and 60 feet, changed at the time of writing to 100, 75, and 50 feet. 'The top was 25 feet above Sam, and above it was the horn-turret, another 50 feet.'[11]

From ' "That's done it!" said Sam. "Now I've rung the front-door bell!" ' a draft text ('C') takes up. This is written in a script so difficult that a good deal of it would be barely comprehensible had it not been closely followed in the fair copy D.[12] The final story was now reached, and there is little to record of these texts. At the point in the narrative where Sam climbed up to the roof of the third (topmost) tier of the Tower there is a little diagram in D showing the form of the open space (not clearly seen in the drawing reproduced on p. 19): rectangular at the base but with the sides drawing together to a point (cf. the 'pointed bastions' referred to in the description of the Tower), roughly in the shape of a haystack. To the statement that the stairhead was 'covered by a small domed chamber in the midst of the roof, with low doors facing east and west' D adds 'Both were open': this was omitted in the second manuscript ('E'), perhaps inadvertently. The name of the sole surviving orc beside Shagrat is *Radbug* in both C and D (*Snaga* in RK; see LR Appendix F, p. 409), *Radbug* being retained in the final story as the name of an orc whose eyes Shagrat says that he had squeezed out (RK p. 182); in C the orcs whom Sam saw running from the gate and shot down as they fled are *Lughorn* and *Ghash* > *Muzgash* (*Lagduf* and *Muzgash* in D, as in RK). Where in RK Snaga declares that 'the great fighter' (Sam) is 'one of those bloody-handed Elves, or one of the filthy *tarks*', and that his getting past the Watchers is '*tark's* work',[13] C has 'that's Elvish work'; D has 'one of these filthy wizards maybe' and 'that's wizard's work' ('wizard' being changed in pencil to '*tark*', which appears in the second manuscript E as written).

Only in one point does the story as told in the draft C differ from that in D. When Gorbag rouses himself from among the corpses on the roof Sam sees in the latter, as in RK (p. 183), that he has in his hand 'a broad-headed spear with a short broken haft'; in C on the other hand he has 'a red [?and shining] sword. It was his own sword, the one he

left by Frodo.' With this cf. text B (p. 25 and note 9): 'Frodo has to
have orc-weapons. The sword is gone.'

Sam's song as he sat on the stair in the horn-turret was much
worked on.[14] I give it here in the form that it has in D, which was
preceded by rougher but closely similar versions.

> I sit upon the stones alone;
>   the fire is burning red,
> the tower is tall, the mountains dark;
>   all living things are dead.
> In western lands the sun may shine,
>   there flower and tree in spring
> is opening, is blossoming:
>   and there the finches sing.
>
> But here I sit alone and think
>   of days when grass was green,
> and earth was brown, and I was young:
>   they might have never been.
> For they are past, for ever lost,
>   and here the shadows lie
> deep upon my heavy heart,
>   and hope and daylight die.
>
> But still I sit and think of you;
>   I see you far away
> Walking down the homely roads
>   on a bright and windy day.
> It was merry then when I could run
>   to answer to your call,
> could hear your voice or take your hand;
>   but now the night must fall.
> And now beyond the world I sit,
>   and know not where you lie!
> O master dear, will you not hear
>   my voice before we die?

The second verse was altered on the manuscript:

> For they are gone, for ever lost,
>   and buried here I lie
> and deep beneath the shadows sink
>   where hope and daylight die.

At the same time the last two lines of the song became:

> O Master, will you hear my voice
>   and answer ere we die?

In this form the song appears in the second manuscript E. At a later stage it was rewritten on this manuscript to become virtually a different song, but still retaining almost unchanged the second half of the original first verse, which now became the opening lines:

> *In western lands the Sun may shine;*
> *there flower and tree in Spring*
> *are opening, are blossoming,*
> *and there the finches sing.*

Further correction of these lines on the manuscript produced the final form (RK p. 185).

A last point concerns the ladder: 'Suddenly the answer dawned on Sam: the topmost chamber was reached by a trap-door in the roof of the passage', RK p. 185. In my account of the fair copy manuscript of 'The Choices of Master Samwise' I did not describe a development in the last words of Shagrat and Gorbag that Sam overheard before they passed through the under-gate of the Tower (TT p. 351). In the draft text, only Shagrat speaks:

> 'Yes, up to the top chamber,' Shagrat was saying, 'right at the top. No way down but by the narrow stair from the Look-out Room below. He'll be safe there.'

In the fair copy this was retained, but Shagrat begins 'Yes, that'll do' (as if the suggestion had come from Gorbag), and 'the ladder' was substituted for 'the narrow stair'. It is thus seen that this element in the story was already present when Book IV was completed. The further development in the conversation of the orcs, in which Gorbag argues against Shagrat's proposal, and Shagrat declares that he does not trust all of his own 'lads', nor any of Gorbag's, nor Gorbag himself (and does not mention that the topmost chamber was reached by ladder), was added to the first typescript of 'The Choices of Master Samwise' at this time, as is seen from the fact that rough drafting for it is found on a page carrying drafts for passages for 'The Land of Shadow'. Curiously, my father wrote at the head of this: 'No way up but by a ladder', as if this idea had only now emerged.[15]

NOTES

1   When Sam came back to the stone door of the orc-passage 'on the inner side he found the catch' (whereas in RK he could not find it and had to climb over). This was retained in the second draft B.

2   For earlier names of the Towers of the Teeth see the Index to *The War of the Ring*, entries *Naglath Morn*, *Nelig Myrn*. The name *Nargos* here is a reversion to one of the original names (*Gorgos* and *Nargos*) of the towers guarding Kirith Ungol, when that was

still the name of the chief pass into Mordor: see VII.344 and note 41.

3   These two orcs, who survived into the final text (RK p. 178), originally appeared in outline IV (p. 9) as messengers sent to Barad-dûr. At that time there was no suggestion that they did not make good their errand.

4   At this stage, presumably, 'The Pyre of Denethor' and 'The Houses of Healing' constituted the two parts of Chapter XLIX (VIII.386), while the remainder of Book V was divided between L and LI (the fair copy manuscript of 'The Black Gate Opens' is numbered LI).

5   In the event, of course, Frodo did not fight, and no draft of this period suggests that he did. Possibly at this stage, before he had come to write the new story of the rescue of Frodo, my father was still thinking in terms of the original plot in 'The Story Foreseen from Lórien', when Frodo was more active (VII.335 ff.).

6   In the fair copy manuscript of 'The Choices of Master Samwise' Sam asked himself: 'How many are there? Thirty, forty, or more?' The change to 'Thirty of forty from the tower at least, and a lot more than that from down below, I guess' (TT p. 344) was made on the first typescript of the chapter. – In outline IV (p. 9) the orcs of the Tower are the more numerous.

7   Cf. the original conception of the Sentinels guarding the entrance to Minas Morgul in 'The Story Foreseen from Lórien' written years before (VII.340–1): 'It was as if some will denying the passage was drawn like invisible ropes across his path. He felt the pressure of unseen eyes. ... The Sentinels sat there: dark and still. They did not move their clawlike hands laid on their knees, they did not move their shrouded heads in which no faces could be seen ...' See also the diagrammatic sketch of the Sentinels in VII.348.

8   The illegible word might possibly be *jewel* (i.e. the brooch of his elven-cloak).

9   *The sword is gone:* this is Sam's sword from the Barrow-downs; cf. 'The Choices of Master Samwise' (TT p. 340): ' "If I'm to go on," he said, "then I must take your sword, by your leave, Mr. Frodo, but I'll put this one to lie by you, as it lay by the old king in the barrow ..." ' See pp. 26–7.

10   This passage concerning their provision of food and water is marked to stand earlier – no doubt after the words 'They make their plans'. The illegible words in the sentence following 'Food. Drink.' could conceivably be read as *stick thrust*, i.e. 'They had found Frodo's sack and stick thrust in corner, rummaged.'

11   A few other differences of detail are worth recording. Where in RK (p. 176) the text reads: 'not even the black shadows, lying deep where the red glow could not reach, would shield him long

from the night-eyed orcs' D continues: 'that were moving to and fro.' This was taken up from the draft B, and remained into the second manuscript of the chapter (E), where it was removed. – Sam's rejection of the temptation to claim the Ring as his own was expressed thus: 'The one small garden of a free gardener was all his need and due, not a garden swollen to a realm; his own hands to command, not the hands of others. Service given with love was his nature, not to command service, whether by fear or in proud benevolence.' – After the words 'He was not really in any doubt' (RK p. 177) there follows in D: 'but he was lonely and he was not used to it, or to acting on his own.' To this my father subsequently added, before striking it all out, 'Since no one else was there he had to talk to himself.'

12   Some passages are absent from the draft C, but not I think because pages are lost: rather D becomes here the initial narrative composition. Thus the passage in RK p. 181 from 'Up, up he went' to ' "Curse you, Snaga, you little maggot" ' is missing; and here the D text becomes notably rougher and full of corrections in the act of writing. The very rough draft C stops near the beginning of Sam's conversation with Frodo in the topmost chamber (RK p. 187), and from that point there are only isolated passages of drafting extant; but the latter part of D was much corrected in the act of writing, and was probably now to a large extent the primary composition.

13   Cf. LR Appendix F (RK p. 409): in Orkish Westron 'tark, "man of Gondor", was a debased form of tarkil, a Quenya word used in Westron for one of Númenorean descent'.

14   For my father's original ideas for the song that Sam sang in this predicament see VII.333.

15   When Frodo and Sam passed out through the gate of the Tower Frodo cried: Alla elenion ancalima! Alla was not changed to Aiya until the book was in type (cf. VIII.223, note 29).

III

THE LAND OF SHADOW

It seems plain that 'The Land of Shadow' was achieved swiftly and in a single burst of writing; the draft material (here compendiously called 'A') consists largely of very roughly written passages immediately transferred to and developed in the first continuous manuscript ('B'), which was given the number 'LIII' (see p. 25) and the title 'Mount Doom', subsequently changed to 'The Land of Shadow'. Only in a few passages did my father go momentarily down an unsuccessful turn in the story.

The first of these concerns the overhearing by Sam and Frodo of the conversation of orcs in the valley beneath the Morgai, which was at first conceived very differently from the story in RK (pp. 202–3). The draft text A is here, as throughout, exceedingly difficult to read.

Presently [three >] two orcs came into view. They were in black without tokens and were armed with bows, a small breed, black-skinned with wide snuffling nostrils, evidently trackers of some kind. .... they were talking in some hideous unintelligible speech; but as they passed snuffling among the stones scarcely 20 yards from where the hobbits lurked Frodo saw that one was carrying on his arm a black mail-shirt very like the one that he had abandoned. He sniffed it as [he] went as if to recall its scent. All at once lifting his head he let out a cry. It was answered, and from the other direction (from Kirith Ungol now some miles behind) ... large fighting orcs came up with shields .... [?painted] with the Eye.

A [?babble] of talk in the common tongue now broke out. 'Nar,' said the tracker, 'not a trace further along. Nor o' this smell, but we're not [?easy]. Somebody that has no business here has been about. Different smell, but a bad smell: we've lost that too, it went up into the mountains.'

'A lot of use you little snufflers are,' grunted a bigger orc. 'I reckon eyes are better than your snotty noses. Have you seen anything?'

'What's to look for?' grunted the tracker.

Amid much further orcish dissension in confused drafting the final story emerges, with two orcs only, a soldier and a small tracker: my

father had some trouble in deciding which offensive remark belonged
to which speaker.

Drafting for the passage in which Sam described to Frodo all that
had happened (RK p. 204) runs thus:

When he had finished Frodo said nothing for some time, but
took Sam's hand and pressed it. At length he stirred. 'So this is
what comes of eavesdropping, Sam,' he said. 'But I wonder if
you'll ever get back. Perhaps it would have been safer to have
been turned into a toad as Gandalf threatened. Do you remember that day, Sam,' he said, 'and clipping the edges under the
window?'

'I do, Mr. Frodo. And I bet things are in [a] nasty mess there
now with [?that] Lobelia and her Cosimo,[1] begging your
pardon. There'll be trouble if ever we get back.'

'I shouldn't worry about that if I were you,' said Frodo.
'We've got to go on again now. East, East, Sam, not West. I
wonder how long it will be before we are caught and all this
slinking and toiling will be over?'

It is curious that Sam, speaking darkly of the state of affairs in the
Shire, should ascribe it to Lobelia and Cosimo Sackville-Baggins. In
the original sketch of the Mirror of Lothlórien, when it was King
Galdaran's Mirror, and when it was Frodo who saw the visions of the
Shire, he was to see 'Cosimo Sackville-Baggins very rich, buying up
land'; but there is no mention of Cosimo in the first narrative of the
scene (VII.249, 253).

Frodo's entrusting of Sting and the Phial of Galadriel to Sam entered
in the first manuscript (B) in this form:

'You must keep the Lady's gift for me, Sam,' he said, 'I've
nowhere to store it now, except in my hand, and I need both in
the dark. And you must keep Sting too, since I have lost your
sword. I have got an orc-blade, but I do not think it is my part to
strike any blows again.'

It was at this time, as it appears, that my father came to a new
perception of the lands in the north-western extremity of Mordor, and
saw that the vale behind the Morannon was closed also at the
southward end by great spurs that thrust out from Ephel Dúath and
Ered Lithui. As first written in B, Frodo told Sam this concerning his
knowledge of Mordor (cf. RK p. 204):

'No very clear notion, Sam,' said Frodo. 'In Rivendell before I
set out I saw old maps made before the Dark Lord came back

here, and I remember them vaguely. I had a little secret plan with names and distances: it was given to me by Elrond, but that has gone with all my other things. I think it was ten leagues or even a dozen from the Bridge to the Narrows, a point where the western and northern ranges send out spurs and make a sort of gate to the deep valley that lies behind the Morannon. The Mountain stands out alone on the plain, but nearer the northern range. Nearly fifty miles I think from the Narrows, more, of course, if we have to keep to the edge of the hills on the other side.'

In a revised version of this Frodo says: 'I guess, not counting our wasted climb, we've done say [twenty miles >] six or seven leagues north from the Bridge since we started.' The final version in this manuscript gives seven leagues as the distance they have traversed, 'ten leagues or so' from the Bridge to the meeting of the mountain-spurs, and still fifty miles from there to Mount Doom. In RK these distances are twelve leagues, not seven; twenty leagues, not ten; and sixty miles, not fifty: see further the Note on Geography at the end of this chapter.

When Frodo and Sam at last set eyes on the north-western confines of Mordor as seen from the south (RK p. 205) the names *Durthang* and *Carach Angren 'the Iron Jaws'* appear in the original draft, but the valley behind Carach Angren is named *the Narch*.[2] The draft text is here partly illegible, but enough can be read to show that the landscape was perfectly clear to my father's eyes as soon as he reached this point in the narrative. In the B text the name *Isenmouthe* appears, though the valley behind is still called 'the deep dark valley of Narch.'[3]

A notable feature in the original draft of the story is that there is no mention of Gollum (see RK p. 206). While Frodo slept Sam went off by himself and found water, as in RK, but then 'the rest of that grey day passed without incident. Frodo slept for [?hours]. Sam did not wake him, but trusting once more to "luck" slept for a long while beside him.' Gollum enters in the B text in these words:

At that moment he thought he caught a glimpse of a black form or shadow flitting among the stones above, near to Frodo's hiding. He was almost back to his master before he was sure. There was Gollum indeed! If his will could have given him strength for a great bound Sam would have sprung straight on his enemy's back; but at that moment Gollum became aware of him and looked back. Sam had a quick glimpse of two pale eyes now filled with a mad malevolent light, and then Gollum, jumping from rock to rock with great agility, fled away onto the ridge and vanished over its crest.

The end of the chapter, the story of Frodo and Sam being forced to join the orc-band coming down from Durthang and their escape from it in the confusion at the road-meeting near the Isenmouthe, was achieved in all but minor details unhesitatingly.[4]

NOTES

1 For Cosimo Sackville-Baggins, later Lotho, see VI.283, VII.32.
2 It was while working on the latter part of 'The Land of Shadow' that my father first mapped this new conception of the north-western extremity of Mordor, on a slip of paper that bears on the reverse drafting for the story of the forced march of Frodo and Sam in the troop of orcs moving from Durthang to the Isen-mouthe. On this little sketch-map the closed vale between the Morannon and the Isenmouthe is named *The Narch*, subsequently overwritten *Udûn*. In my description of the Second Map in VIII.438 I noted that the vale was first marked *Gorgoroth*, but that this was struck out, 'and in its place was pencilled here the name *Narch Udûn*.' It is in fact clear that *Narch* alone was first written, and that *Udûn* was intended as a replacement.
3 This was changed later to 'the deep dale of Kirith Gorgor', and then to 'the deep dale of Udûn' (see note 2).
4 A few such details from the earliest form of the conclusion of the chapter may be mentioned. The orc 'slave-drivers' are called 'two of the large fierce *uruks*, the fighting-orcs', and this seems to be the first time that the word was used (though the name *Uruk-hai* had appeared long since, VII.409, VIII.22, see also p. 436); and it is said that 'one of the slave-drivers *with night-sighted eyes* spied the two figures by the roadside.' Where in RK this orc says 'All your folk should have been inside Udûn before yesterday evening' he says here 'inside the Narch-line'; and following his words 'Don't you know we're at war?' he adds: 'If the elvish folk get the best of it, they won't treat you so kindly.'

Note on the Geography

In the first draft of the chapter, when Frodo and Sam climbed to the crest of the Morgai and looking out eastwards saw Mount Doom, it was 'still 30 miles away, perhaps, due East from where the hobbits stood.' In the B text, in the following manuscript, and in the final typescript for the printer, the distance became 'seven leagues or more', and was only altered to 'forty miles at least' (RK p. 200) at a late stage. It is impossible to relate '30 miles', still less 'seven leagues', to any of the maps. On the Second Map the distance due East from the Morgai to Mount Doom (in its second, more westerly, position, see VIII.438) is just under 50 miles, while on the Third Map (the last general small-scale map that my father made) it became 80 miles. On the large-scale map of Rohan, Gondor and Mordor the distance is somewhat under 60 miles, as Mount Doom was first placed; but when it was moved further to the west it became about 43 miles (under 40 in my redrawing of the map published in *The Return of the King*), with which the text of RK agrees.

The distance from the Morgai bridge below Kirith Ungol to the Isenmouthe was roughly estimated from memory by Frodo (p. 33) as 'ten leagues or even a dozen' (30–36 miles); and 'ten leagues at least' remained into the final typescript before being changed to the figure in RK (p. 204), 'twenty leagues at least'. The Second Map does not allow of precise measurement of the distance from the Morgai bridge to the Isenmouthe, since the conception of the closing of the vale behind the Morannon by spurs of Ephel Dúath and Ered Lithui had not arisen when it was made, but it could be minimally calculated as between 30 and 40 miles; on the large-scale map it becomes 56 miles or just under 19 leagues, agreeing with the twenty leagues of RK.

Frodo's estimation of the distance from the Isenmouthe to Mount Doom as about fifty miles likewise remained through all the texts until replaced at the very end by sixty. This distance is roughly 50 miles on the Second Map, about 80 on the Third Map, and 62 on the large-scale map as Mount Doom was first placed; when it was moved further west the distance from the Isenmouthe became 50 miles. The change of 50 to 60 at the end of the textual history of RK is thus, strangely, the reverse of the development of the map.

In the original draft Sam and Frodo joined the road to the Isenmouthe 'after it had already run down some 4 miles from the orc-hold of Durthang and turned away somewhat northward so that the long descent behind was hidden from them [?hurrying] on the stony road. They had been going an hour and had covered perhaps some 3 miles without meeting any enemy when they heard what they had all along dreaded ...' In B 'they came at last to the road where, after descending swiftly from Durthang, it became more level and ran under the ridge towards the Isenmouthe, a distance of perhaps ten miles.' As in A, they had only been on the road for an hour when they were overtaken by the orcs, and it is added in B at this point 'it was maybe six miles yet before the road would leave its high shelf and go down into the plain.' In the following manuscript and in the final typescript for the printer the hobbits still reached the road 'at the point where it swung east towards the Isenmouthe ten miles away', and it was still after only an hour on the road that they halted, and were shortly afterwards overtaken. On the typescript my father emended 'ten miles' to 'twenty miles', and 'an hour' to 'three hours', but the final reading of RK was 'after doing some twelve miles, they halted.' On the large-scale map the track of Frodo and Sam up the valley below the Morgai is marked, and the point where their track joined the road from Durthang is 20 miles from the Isenmouthe; the change in the text was thus very probably made to accommodate it to the map. The change whereby the hobbits had gone for three hours or twelve miles along the road before being overtaken clearly followed from the increased distance to the Isenmouthe, in order to reduce the time that Frodo and Sam had to submit to the punishing pace set by the orcs before they escaped.

Note on the Chronology

Dates are written in the margins of the original texts of this chapter. At this stage the chronology of the journey from Kirith Ungol can be set out thus:

March 14   Dawn: Frodo and Sam climb down into the valley below the Morgai. Wind changes and the darkness begins to be driven back.
  Night of March 14–15: They sleep below the crest of the Morgai; Sam sees a star.
March 15   They reach the top of the Morgai and see Mount Doom; descend and continue up the valley; overhear the two orcs quarrelling.
  Night of March 15–16: They continue up the valley northward.
March 16   They spend the day in hiding in the valley.
  Night of March 16–17: They continue up the valley.
March 17   In hiding. They see Durthang and the road descending from it. Gollum reappears.
  Night of March 17–18: They take the road from Durthang and are forced to join the orc-company.

This chronology accords with the date March 14 of the Battle of the Pelennor Fields (see VIII.428–9); in both the drafting A and the first manuscript B of the chapter 'It was the morning of the fourteenth of March ... Théoden lay dying on the Pelennor Fields.' Here in RK (p. 196) it was the morning of March 15; and all the dates as given above are in the final story one day later.

IV

MOUNT DOOM

The original draft of the chapter 'Mount Doom' was written continuously with the first completed manuscript B of 'The Land of Shadow', which at this stage was called 'Mount Doom' (see p. 31); but the division into two chapters was soon made.

The latter part of the original single chapter (which I will continue to call 'B') is remarkable in that the primary drafting constitutes a completed text, with scarcely anything in the way of preparatory sketching of individual passages, and while the text is rough and full of corrections made at the time of composition it is legible almost throughout; moreover many passages underwent only the most minor changes later. It is possible that some more primitive material has disappeared, but it seems to me far more probable that the long thought which my father had given to the ascent of Mount Doom and the destruction of the Ring enabled him, when at last he came to write it, to achieve it more quickly and surely than almost any earlier chapter in *The Lord of the Rings*. He had known from far back (see p. 3) that when Frodo (still called 'Bingo') came to the Crack of Doom he would be unable to cast away the Ring, and that Gollum would take it and fall into the chasm. But how did he fall? In subsequent outlines Sam's part was pondered. My father knew that Sam was attacked by Gollum on the way up the Mountain and delayed, so that Frodo made the final ascent alone; and he knew that Gollum got hold of the Ring by taking Frodo's finger with it. But for a long time he thought that it was Sam who, finally making his way to the Chamber of Fire, pushed Gollum with the Ring into the abyss. In none of the later outlines given in Chapter I did he achieve the final articulation of the story; but there seems good reason to think that these belong to the period of the writing of Book V, and if my chronological deductions are correct (see pp. 12–13), he had had plenty of time to 'find out what really happened' before he came actually to describe the final moments of the Quest.

As I have said, the final form of 'Mount Doom' was quite largely achieved in the first draft (B), and I give the following brief passage (interesting also for another reason) as exemplification (cf. RK p. 223):

'Master!' he cried. Then Frodo stirred, and spoke with a clear voice, indeed a voice clearer and more powerful than Sam had ever heard him use, and it rose above the throb and turmoils of the chasm of Mount Doom, echoing in the roof and walls.

'I have come,' he said. 'But I cannot do what I have come to do. I will not do it. The Ring is mine.' And suddenly he vanished from Sam's sight. Sam gasped, but at that moment many things happened. Something struck Sam violently in the back, his legs were knocked from under him and he was flung aside striking his head against the stony floor. He lay still.

And far away as Frodo put on the Ring the Power in Baraddur was shaken and the Tower trembled from its foundations to its proud and bitter crown. The Dark Lord was suddenly aware of him, the Eye piercing all shadows looked across the plain to the door in Orodruin, and all the plot [> devices] was laid bare to it. Its wrath blazed like a sudden flame and its fear was like a great black smoke, for it knew its deadly peril, the thread upon which hung its doom. From all its policies and webs its mind shook free, and through all its realm a tremor ran, its slaves quailed, and its armies halted and its captains suddenly steerless bereft of will wavered and despaired. But its thought was now bent with all its overwhelming force upon the Mountain; and at its summons wheeling with a ...ing cry in a last desperate race there flew, faster than the wind, the Nazgûl, the Ringwraiths, with a storm of wings they hurtled towards Mount Doom.

Frodo's words 'But *I cannot do* what I have come to do' were changed subsequently on the B-text to 'But *I do not choose now to do* what I have come to do.' I do not think that the difference is very significant, since it was already a central element in the outlines that Frodo would *choose* to keep the Ring himself; the change in his words does no more than emphasize that he fully willed his act. (In the second text of the chapter, the fair copy manuscript 'C',[1] Sam cried out just before this not merely 'Master!' as in the first text and in RK but 'Master! Do it quick!' – these words being bracketed probably at the time of setting them down.)

This passage is notable in showing the degree to which my father had come to identify the Eye of Barad-dûr with the mind and will of Sauron, so that he could speak of 'its wrath, its fear, its thought'. In the second text C he shifted from 'its' to 'his' as he wrote out this passage anew.

Some other differences in the original text are worth recording. On the morning after they escaped from the orc-band marching to the Isenmouthe, following Frodo's words 'I can manage it. I must' (RK p. 211) text B at first continued:

In the end they decided to crawl in such cover as they could towards the north-range [and then turn south >] until they were further from the vigilance on the ramparts, and then turn south.

As they went from hollow to hollow or along cracks in the stony ground, keeping always if they could some screen between them and the north, they saw that the most easterly of the three roads went also in the same direction. It was in fact the road to the Dark Tower, as Frodo guessed.

He looked at it. 'I shall wear myself out in a day of this crawling and stooping,' he said. 'If we are to go on we must risk it. We must take the road.'

Here my father stopped, struck this out, and replaced it by a passage very close to that in RK, where it is Sam who sees that they can go no further in this fashion and must risk taking the road to the Dark Tower.

Another slight difference in the original text follows Frodo's words to Sam on the morning on which they left the road and turned south towards Mount Doom: 'I can't manage it, Sam. It is such a weight to carry, such a weight' (RK p. 214).

Sam knew what he meant, but seeking for some encouragement amid despair he answered: 'Well, Mr Frodo, why not lighten the load a bit. We're going that way as straight as we can make.' He pointed to the Mountain. 'No good taking anything we're not sure to need.'

Like a child, distracted from its trouble by some game of make-believe, Frodo considered his words seriously for a moment. Then 'Of course,' he said. 'Leave everything behind we don't want. Travel light, that's the thing, Sam!' He picked up his orc-shield and flung it away, and threw his helmet after it; and undoing his heavy belt cast it and the sword and sheath with it clattering on the ground. Even his grey cloak he threw away.

Sam looked at him with pity.

This was struck out immediately and replaced by the text of RK, in which Sam suggests that he should bear the Ring for a while. But neither in the text B nor in the fair copy C is there mention of the phial of Galadriel or of the little box that she gave to Sam.[2]

The height of Mount Doom was at first differently conceived: 'It was indeed some 3000 feet or so from foot to the .... broken crater at its crown. A third of that height now lay below him ...' Text C still differs from RK (p. 218): 'The confused and tumbled shoulders of its great sprawling base rose for maybe three[3] thousand feet above the plain, and above them was reared, *almost as high again*, its tall central cone, like a vast oast or chimney capped by a jagged crater. But already Sam stood *half way up* the base ...' (where RK has 'half as high again' and 'more than half way up'). My father's drawing, reproduced in *Pictures by J. R. R. Tolkien* no. 30, and in this book on p. 42, from a small page that carries also a scrap of drafting for this part of the chapter, seems to show the final conception, with the cone 'half as high again' in relation to the 'base'; but in this drawing the door of the Sammath Naur is at the foot of the cone, whereas in all versions of the text the climbing road came 'high in the upper cone, but still far from the reeking summit, to a dark entrance'.[4]

When Gollum fell upon Sam as he carried Frodo up the road, both in the original text and in the fair copy C Sam not only tore the backs of his hands as he crashed forward (RK p. 220) but also cut his forehead on the ground. In B, against the words 'But Sam gave him no more heed. He suddenly remembered his master. He looked up the path and could not see him' (RK p. 222) my father wrote in the margin: 'his head was bleeding?' This was not taken up in C, but a little earlier, after the words 'Sam's hand wavered. His mind was hot with wrath and the memory of evil' (RK p. 221) C has: 'Blood trickled down his forehead.' Both these references to Sam's bleeding forehead were later struck from C. It is not clear to me what my father had in mind here. At first sight there might seem to be a connection with Sam's blindness in outline V (p. 11): 'Sam feels a blindness coming on and wonders if it is due to water of Mordor ... Sam half-blind is lagging behind', but that seems to have been introduced to explain how it was that when Gollum attacked Frodo went on unaware of what had happened; whereas here the blood in Sam's eyes was the result of Gollum's attack, and he himself urged Frodo to go on. Possibly the cutting of his forehead was intended to explain why Sam could not see Frodo when he looked up the path, and was removed when my father came to the point when Sam was again felled by Gollum in the Sammath Naur: 'He was dazed, and blood streaming from his head dripped in his eyes' (RK p. 223).

When Sam urged Frodo to go on up alone while he dealt with Gollum Frodo replied, both in B and C: 'The Quest shall now be all fulfilled', where in RK he said: 'This is the end at last.'

At the end of the chapter, after the words 'Down like lashing whips fell a torrent of black rain' (RK p. 224), the first text moves at once to ' "Well, this is the end, Sam," said a voice by his side.' Here my father wrote in the margin soon after: 'Put in here (or in next chapter?) vision of the cloudwrack out of Baraddur [?growing] to shape of a vast black [?man] that stretches out a menacing unavailing arm and is blown away.' The word 'man' is very unclear but I cannot see how else it could be read. Later at this point in the manuscript he wrote 'Fall of Ringwraiths' with a mark of insertion, and the passage 'And into the heart of the storm, with a cry that pierced all other sounds ...' appears in C.

Lastly, Sam's feelings were thus described in B: 'If he felt anything in all that ruin of the world, it was perhaps most of all a great joy, to be servant once again, and know his master [added: and surrender to him the leadership].' This was repeated in C, but rejected and replaced by the reading of RK. In Frodo's final words he did not, in the original text, speak of forgiving Gollum.[5]

NOTES

1 The fair copy manuscript C is entitled 'Mount Doom' and numbered 'LIV' (see pp. 31, 37), the number changed subsequently to 'LII' (see p. 25).

2 Sam's vain use of the Phial when he entered the Sammath Naur (RK p. 222) appears in B. The addition concerning the Phial and the box was made later to text C.

   The passage in which Sam remembered paddling in the Pool at Bywater with the children of Farmer Cotton (RK p. 216) is also absent from B. This is one of the few passages in this chapter for which a separate draft is found (before its introduction into text C), and here the names of the Cotton children are seen emerging.

3 *three* was changed in pencil to *two* on the manuscript (C), but *three* survived.

4 In both B and C, despite the earlier statement (as in RK p. 219) that the road came 'high in the upper cone ... to a dark entrance', it is said in the passage corresponding to that in RK p. 222 that the road 'with a last course passed *across the base of the cone* and came to the dark door', where in RK 'with a last eastward course [it] passed *in a cutting along the face of the cone* and came to the dark door'.

   In B there is a little sketch of Mount Doom which my father struck through, and here the entrance to the Sammath Naur is placed about a third of the way up the cone (which is here shorter in relation to the base than in the drawing reproduced on p. 42). The road here disappears round the eastern side of the cone, below the door, and seems (the drawing is hard to make out) to reappear further up, coming from the left (east) and ending at the door.

5 A couple of points concerning names in this chapter may be mentioned. In the opening paragraph both B and C have 'He heard the scuffling and cries die down as the troops passed on into the Narch', where RK has 'passed on through the Isenmouthe'; see p. 33. The name *Sammath Naur* does not appear in B, but enters in C without any initial hesitation as to its form.

Mount Doom

Note on the Chronology

The chronology was still a day behind that of RK (see p. 36). At nightfall of the day on which they escaped from the orc-band at the Isenmouthe my father wrote in the margin of text B '18 ends'; this was March 19 in RK (in *The Tale of Years* 'Frodo and Samwise escape and begin their journey along the road to the Barad-dûr'). The reference to the passing of the Cross Roads by the Captains of the West and the burning of the fields of Imlad Morghul (so spelt) is however present in B at the same point as in RK (p. 212): see VIII.432.

In B, against the words 'There came at last a dreadful evening; and even as the Captains of the West drew near the end of the living lands, the two wanderers came to an hour of blank despair' (cf. RK p. 212), my father wrote 'end of 22'. This was the same date as in RK, and thus there follows in the original text 'Five days had passed since they escaped the orcs' (i.e. March 18–22), where RK has 'Four'.

V

THE FIELD OF KORMALLEN

In the first draft of this chapter my father again achieved for most of its length an extraordinarily close approach to the final form, and this is the more remarkable when one considers that he had no plan or outline before him. There had been many mentions of a great feast to follow the final victory (VII.212, 345, 448; VIII.275, 397), but nothing had ever been said of it beyond the fact that it was to take place in Minas Tirith.[1] That this text ('A') was indeed the first setting down on paper of the story and that nothing preceded it seems obvious from the nature of the manuscript itself, which has all the marks of primary composition.[2] It was followed by a fair copy manuscript ('B'), bearing the number and title 'LV   The Field of Kormallen', which was also pencilled in later on A.

Not until the end of the minstrel's song of Frodo of the Nine Fingers and the Ring of Doom did the first text A diverge in any narrative point, and little even in expression, from the form in RK. There are however several interesting details.

One of these concerns the Eagles. As the passage (RK p. 226) describing their coming above the Morannon was first written it read:

> There came Gwaihir, the Wind-lord, and Lhandroval his brother, greatest of all the eagles of the north, mightiest of the descendants of [added: Great > old] Thorondor who built his eyries in the immeasurable peaks of Thangorodrim [changed immediately to the Encircling Mountains] when Middle-earth was young.

In the *Quenta* §15 (IV.137) it is told that after the Battle of Unnumbered Tears 'Thorndor King of Eagles removed his eyries from Thangorodrim to the northward heights of the Encircling Mountains [*about the plain of Gondolin*], and there he kept watch, sitting upon the cairn of King Fingolfin.' In the *Quenta Silmarillion* of 1937 there is no mention of the Eagles dwelling on Thangorodrim, and at the time of the fall of Fingolfin in his duel with Morgoth, before the Battle of Unnumbered Tears, Thorondor came for the rescue of the king's body 'from his eyrie among the peaks of Gochressiel' (i.e. the Encircling Mountains; V.285, §147). On the other hand, in the abandoned story 'Of Tuor and the Fall of Gondolin' given in *Unfinished Tales*, a story that I believe to have been written in 1951, Voronwë speaks to Tuor of 'the folk of Thorondor, who dwelt once even on Thangorodrim ere Morgoth grew so mighty, and dwell now in the Mountains of Turgon since the fall of Fingolfin' (p. 43).

Gwaihir the Windlord had of course appeared often before this in *The Lord of the Rings* (for long *Gwaewar*, but becoming *Gwaihir* in the course of the writing of 'The White Rider', VII.430). In the *Quenta Silmarillion* (see V.301) Gwaewar had been one of the three eagles that came to Angband for the rescue of Beren and Lúthien; the earliest form of that passage reads:

Thorondor led them, and the others were Lhandroval (Wide-wing) and Gwaewar his vassal.

The following text (also belonging to 1937) has:

Thorondor was their leader; and with him were his mightiest vassals, wide-winged Lhandroval, and Gwaewar lord of the wind.

In a revision of the passage which can be dated to 1951 *Gwaewar* was changed to *Gwaihir*. As I have noticed in V.301, the names of the vassals of Thorondor were suppressed in the published *Silmarillion* (p. 182) on account of the present passage in RK, but this was certainly mistaken: it is clear that my father deliberately repeated the names. As in so many other cases in *The Lord of the Rings*, he took the name *Gwaewar* for the great eagle, friend of Gandalf, from *The Silmarillion*, and when *Gwaihir* replaced *Gwaewar* in *The Lord of the Rings* he made the same change to the eagle's name in *The Silmarillion*. Now he took also *Lhandroval*[3] to be the name of Gwaihir's brother; and added a new name, *Meneldor* (RK p. 228).

At the fall of the Black Gate Gandalf said only: 'The Realm of Sauron is ended'; but to this my father added, probably immediately: 'So passes the Third Age of the World.' This was placed within brackets, and 'The Ringbearer has fulfilled his Quest' written in the margin.

To Gwaihir Gandalf said: 'You will not find me a burden any greater than when you bore me from Zirakinbar where my old life burned away.' *Zirakinbar* remained through all the texts of the chapter and was only changed to *Zirakzigil* on the galley proof. On these names see VII.174 and 431 with note 6.

Another difference in A which survived long (into the final typescript of the chapter) was the absence of Sam's expression of astonishment at seeing Gandalf at his bedside ('Gandalf! I thought you were dead! But then I thought I was dead myself. . . .', RK p. 230).

The date of the Field of Kormallen (as the name was spelt until the final typescript) was expressed by Gandalf thus in A:

'Noon?' said Sam, puzzling his brains. 'Noon of what day?'

'The third day of the New Year,' said Gandalf, 'or if you like the twenty-eighth day of March in the Shire-reckoning. But in Gondor the New Year will always begin upon the 25th of March when Sauron fell, and when you were brought out of the fire to the King. ...'[4]

If March 25th was New Year's Day, the 28th was the fourth day of the New Year in Gondor, and my father wrote 'fourth' above 'third', without however striking out 'third'. In pencil he wrote 'seventh' against this, and 'the last day' above 'the twenty-eighth day', although this would give 31 days to the month. His reason for this is obscurely indicated by a note in the margin: 'More time required for [?gathering] of goods, say' (i.e., 'say the seventh').[5]

In the fair copy B as written Gandalf said 'The Seventh of the New Year; or if you like, the last day of March in the Shire-reckoning'; this was changed later to 'The Fourteenth of the New Year' and 'the sixth day of April in the Shire-reckoning'. Even allowing 31 days to the month, the sixth of April would be the thirteenth day of the New Year, and 'sixth' was afterwards changed to 'seventh', and finally to 'eighth', as in RK. I do not know precisely what considerations impelled my father so greatly to prolong the time during which Sam and Frodo lay asleep.

Their first conversation with Gandalf ends thus in A:

'What shall we wear?' said Sam, for all he could see were the old and tattered clothes that they had journeyed in, lying folded on the ground beside their beds.

'The clothes that you were found in,' said Gandalf. 'No silks and linen, nor any armour or heraldry, could be more honourable. But afterwards we shall see.'

This survived through all the texts to the galley, where 'The clothes that you were found in' was changed to 'The clothes that you journeyed in'. It was not until the Second Edition of 1966 that the passage was altered and extended, by changing Gandalf's words to 'The clothes that you wore on your way to Mordor.[6] Even the orc-rags that you bore in the black land, Frodo, shall be preserved', and by his return of the Phial of Galadriel and the box that she gave to Sam (RK pp. 230–1; cf. p. 39 and note 2).

The crying of praise as Frodo and Sam came to the Field of Kormallen underwent many changes. In all the texts of the chapter Old English phrases cried by the Riders of Rohan were mingled. The form of the 'Praise' in A runs thus (with some punctuation added from the B-text, which is closely similar):

Long live the halflings! Praise them with great praise! Cuio i Pheriannath anann, aglar anann! Praise them with great praise!

Hale, hale cumath, wesath hale awa to aldre. Fróda and Samwís! Praise them! Kuivië, kuivië! laurea'esselínen![7] *Praise them!*

In the fair copy B the Old English words were changed to *Wilcuman, wilcuman, Fróda and Samwís!* and the Quenya words became *Laitalle, laitalle, andave laita!* In the first typescript the Old English *Uton herian holbytlan!* was added before *Laitalle, laitalle*; and in the second (final) typescript the Quenya words became *A laituvar, laituvar, andave laita!* This was then changed on the typescript to *A laita te, laita te! Andave laituvalme!* Thus the form as it appears on the galley proof is:

> *Long live the Halflings! Praise them with great praise! Cuio i Pheriannath anann! Aglar anann! Praise them with great praise! Wilcuman, wilcuman, Fróda and Samwís! Praise them! Uton herian holbytlan! A laita te, laita te! Andave laituvalmet! Praise them! The Ringbearers, praise them with great praise!*

The final text of the 'Praise', as it appears in RK, was typed onto the galley proof.

From the end of the minstrel's song (RK p. 232) the original text A runs thus:

And then Aragorn stood up and all the host rose, and they passed to a pavilion made ready, there to eat and drink and make merry.

But as Sam and Frodo stepped down with Aragorn from the throne Sam caught sight of a small man-at-arms as it seemed in the silver and sable of the guards of the king: but he was small and he wondered what such a boy was doing in such an army. Then suddenly he exclaimed: 'Why, look Mr Frodo. Look here. Bless me if it's not Pippin, Mr Peregrin Took I should say. Bless me but I can see there's more tales than ours to hear. It'll take weeks before we get it all right.'

'Yes,' said Frodo. 'I can see myself locked up in a room somewhere making notes for days or Bilbo will be bitterly disappointed.'

And so they passed to the feast and at a sign from Aragorn Pippin went with them.[8]

The page carrying this text was rejected; on the back of it is an outline of the story to come (see p. 51, 'The Story Foreseen from Kormallen'). A replacement page was substituted, but again the development turned out to be unsatisfactory:

But first Frodo and Sam were led apart and taken to a tent, and there their old raiment was taken off, but folded and set aside with honour; and clean linen was brought to them. But Gandalf came and with him went an esquire, no more than a small lad he seemed, though clad in the silver and sable of the king's guard, and to the wonder of Frodo and Sam they bore the sword and the elven-cloak and the mithril-coat that had been taken from them; and for Sam they brought a coat of gilded mail, and on Frodo's right hand upon the middle[9] and little fingers they set small rings of mithril set each with a gem like a star. But the wonder of all these things was as little to the wonder on Sam's face as he looked on the face of the esquire and knew him.

And he cried out: 'Why look, Mr. Frodo. Look here! Save me, if it isn't Pippin, Mr. Peregrin Took, I should say. Why bless us all, but I can see there's more tales to tell than ours. It will take weeks of talk before we get it all sized up.'

'It will indeed,' said Pippin. 'But at present it is time for a feast, and you must not keep it waiting. Later on, Frodo must be locked up in a tower in Minas Tirith till he's made notes of all our doings, or Bilbo will be dreadfully disappointed.'

This passage was at once reconstructed to remove Pippin from the scene, and Gandalf comes to the tent alone, as in RK (p. 233). When he has set the rings of mithril on Frodo's fingers the feast follows at once:

... and on Frodo's right hand, upon the middle and little fingers, he set fine rings of mithril, slender as threads of silk but bearing each a small gem shining like a star.[10] And when they were made ready, and circlets of silver were set upon their heads, they went to the feast, and sat with Gandalf, and there was Aragorn and King Éomer of Rohan and all the Captains of the West, and there too were Legolas and Gimli.

[*Struck out at once:* 'That's six of the Company,' said Sam to Frodo. 'Where are the o(thers)] But when wine was brought there came in an esquire to serve the Kings of Gondor and Rohan, or so he seemed, and he was clad in the silver and sable of the guards of the King; but he was small, and Sam wondered what such a boy was doing in an army of mighty men. [*Then follows Sam's recognition of Pippin, as above.*]

'It will indeed,' said Pippin, 'and we'll begin as soon as this feast is ended. In the meantime you can try Gandalf. He's not as close as he used to be, though he laughs now more than he talks.'

And so at last the glad day ended; and when the sun was gone and the crescent moon[11] rode slowly above the mist of Anduin and flickered through the fluttering leaves, Frodo and Sam sat amid the night-fragrance of fair Ithilien, and talked deep into the night with Pippin and Gandalf and Legolas and Gimli.

At last Gandalf rose. 'The hands of the King are hands of healing, dear friends,' he said. 'But you went near to the very brink of death, and though you have slept long and blessedly, still it is now time to rest again. Not you only, Frodo and Sam, but you Peregrin also. For when they lifted you from under the slain it is said that even Aragorn despaired of you.'

Probably at once, this was emended throughout to make Merry also present (see note 8), and the last part of it (Gandalf's parting words) was in turn rejected. In very rough further drafting the final text was approached, though not achieved, in the manuscript A. Gimli's speech (RK p. 234) at this time ended thus:

'... And when I heaved that great carcase off you, then I made sure you were dead. I could have torn out my beard. And that was but a week ago. To bed now you go. And so shall I.'

From this it is seen that it was 'the seventh day of the New Year': see p. 46.[12] The draft continues to its end thus:

'And I,' said Legolas, 'shall walk in the woods of this fair land, which is rest enough. And in days to come, if my Elven lord will allow it, some of our folk shall remove hither, for it is more lovely than any lands they have yet dwelt in;[13] and then it will be blessed for a while. But Anduin is near and Anduin leads down to the sea. To the sea, to the sea, and the white gulls crying, to the sea and the sea and the white foam flying,' and so singing he went away down the hill.

And then the others departed and Frodo and Sam went to their beds and slept; and in the morning the host prepared to return to Minas Tirith. The ships had come and they were lying under Cair Andros, and soon all would be set across the Great River, and so in peace and ease fare over the green swards of Anórien and to the Pelennor and the towers under tall Mindolluin, the city of the men of Gondor, last memory of Westernesse.

Thus the name *Kormallen* did not enter in the original text of the chapter, and it is not said that the Field was near to Henneth Annûn; but scribbled drafting put in later on the last page of the manuscript shows the final text emerging:

And in the morning they rose again and spent many days in Ithilien, for the Field of Kormallen where the host was encamped was near to Henneth Annûn, and they wandered here and there visiting the scenes of their adventures, but Sam lingered ever in some shadow of the woods to find maybe some sight of the Oliphaunt. And when he heard that in the seige of Gondor there had been fifty of them at the least, but all were dead, he thought it a great loss. And in the meanwhile the host rested, for they had laboured much and had fought long and hard against the remnant of the Easterlings and Southrons; and they waited also for those that were to return.

In the fair copy B the final text of the First Edition was present in all but a few points, most of which have been mentioned in the foregoing account and in the notes;[14] but an important change in the description of the dressing of Frodo and Sam before the feast (RK p. 233) was made in the Second Edition. As the text stood in the First Edition (going back unchanged to the fair copy manuscript B) it ran:

... For Sam he brought a coat of gilded mail, and his elven-cloak all healed of the soils and hurts that it had suffered; and when the Hobbits were made ready, and circlets of silver were set upon their heads, they went to the King's feast, and they sat at his table with Gandalf ...

In the Second Edition the passage was added in which Gandalf brought Sting and Sam's sword, and Frodo had to be persuaded to wear a sword and to accept back Sting. At this time also the reference was added to 'the Standing Silence' before the feast began.

NOTES

1   There had been a suggestion (VIII.397) that the tale of the passage of the Paths of the Dead should be told at the 'feast of victory in Minas Tirith', but that idea had of course been overtaken.

2   It may be that the first draft of 'The Field of Kormallen' was written before the fair copy manuscript of 'Mount Doom'. A pointer to this is the fact that where in RK (p. 228) 'a great smoke and steam belched from the Sammath Naur' A has 'a great fire belched from the cave': see p. 41 note 5.

3   The first draft A has the spelling *Lhandroval* at all occurrences, but the fair copy B has *Landroval*, as in RK.

4   Both in A and B it is Frodo who asks 'What king, and who is he?' On the first typescript Sam's question 'What shall we wear?' was transferred to Frodo, but in the final typescript given back to Sam.

5   Perhaps to be compared is the sentence in 'The Steward and the King', RK pp. 241–2: 'Merry was summoned [*from Minas Tirith*] and rode away with the wains that took store of goods to Osgiliath and thence by ship to Cair Andros.'

6   Frodo was naked when Sam found him in the Tower of Kirith Ungol; he had to dress in 'long hairy breeches of some unclean beast-fell, and a tunic of dirty leather' (RK p. 189).

7   *laurea'esselínen* was changed at the time of writing to *ankalim'esselínen*.

8   At this stage, when only a little time had passed since the fall of Sauron, Merry would still have been in Minas Tirith; cf. note 5.

9   My father named the penultimate finger (the 'fourth finger' or 'ring-finger') the 'third finger'; so Frodo's 'third finger was missing' (RK p. 229).

10 The rings of mithril set on Frodo's fingers were retained in the fair copy B, where the passage was struck out.

11 The 'crescent moon' remained in B and in the first typescript, where it was changed to 'the round moon'.

12 It is strange that in B Gimli said here, not as in RK 'And it is only a day yet since you were first up and abroad again', but 'a few days' (this being corrected on the manuscript).

13 This sentence was retained in B and the first typescript, where it was struck out.

14 To these may be added the retention of the name *Narch* in 'And they passed over the Narch and Gorgoroth' (RK p. 228), subsequently emended to *Udûn*. At the end of the chapter it was said at first in B that 'when the month of May was passed seven days the Captains of the West set out again', but this was changed to 'when the month of May was drawing near', and at the same time the last sentence of the chapter was changed from 'for the King would enter his gates with the rising of the Sun' by the addition of the words 'it was the Eve of May, and (the King would enter ...)'.

THE STORY FORESEEN FROM KORMALLEN

This page (see p. 47) was scribbled down in pencil in my father's most impossible handwriting. I have not marked with queries a number of words that I think are probable but not altogether certain, and I have expanded several names given only as initials. The first sentence was written separately from the rest of the outline, whether before or after.

Gimli explains how Pippin was saved.

Next scene – The Host sets out from Cair Andros and [*read* in] the ships and passes into Gondor.

Scene shifts to Merry and to Faramir and Éowyn.

Return of King Elessar. His crowning. His judgements ..... of Berithil.

The hobbits wait. For there is to be a wedding. Elrond and Galadriel and Celeborn come and bring Finduilas.

The wedding of Aragorn and Finduilas.

Also Faramir and Éowyn.

The end of the Third Age is presaged. What the Rings had done. Their power waned. Galadriel and Elrond prepare to depart.

The hobbits return with Éomer to the funeral of Théoden and then on through the Gap of Rohan [?with ..... and the Dúnedain].

They come on Saruman and he is [?pardoned].

They come to Rivendell and see Bilbo. Bilbo gives him Sting and the coat. But he is getting old.

They come back to the Shire [*added in margin:* via Bree, pick up pony] and drive out Cosimo Sackville-Baggins. Lobelia is dead – she had a fit in [?quarrel]. Sam replants the trees. Frodo goes back to Bag End. All is quiet for a year or two. And then one day Frodo takes Sam for a walking [?tour] to the Woody End. And [?behold there go many] Elves. Frodo rides to the Havens and says farewell to Bilbo. End of the Third Age.

Sam's Book.

It is plain that my father wrote this outline while he was working on 'The Field of Kormallen', and indeed the precise stage in that work can probably be deduced: for Gimli's words at the end of the evening, in which he spoke of finding Pippin under the heap of slain, had not entered ('Gimli explains how Pippin was saved'). The precise placing of these notes in the history of the composition of Book VI gives them a particular interest. Several features of the end of the story now appear for the first time: as the marriage of Faramir and Éowyn; Bilbo's giving of the mithril-coat and Sting to Frodo ('forgetting that he had already done so', RK p. 265); the time of peace and quiet after the return of the hobbits to the Shire (but that 'Sam's casket restores Trees' had been known for a long time, VII.286); and Frodo's walk with Sam to the Woody End. But the death, before the return of the hobbits, of Lobelia Sackville-Baggins in a fit (of fury? – the word I have given as *quarrel* is scarcely more than a guess) was not permanent: she would be resurrected, survive her imprisonment during the troubles of the Shire, and end her days in a much more enlightened fashion.

This outline is as elliptical as were so many of my father's sketches of the further course of the story, concentrating on particular elements and ignoring or only hinting at others; and it is hard to know what narrative idea underlay the words 'Frodo rides to the Havens and says farewell to Bilbo'. Many years before (VI.380) he had written that when 'Bingo' returned to the Shire he would make peace, and would then 'settle down in a little hut on the high green ridge – until one day he goes with the Elves west beyond the towers' (cf. also another note of that time, VI.379: 'Island in sea. Take Frodo there in end'). In the outline 'The Story Foreseen from Moria' (VII.212) he had concluded his synopsis thus:

XXVIII What happens to Shire?

    Last scene. Sailing away of Elves [*added:* Bilbo with them] . . .

XXIX Sam and Frodo go into a green land by the Sea?

In another note of that period (VII.287) he said: 'When old, Sam and Frodo set sail to island of West ... Bilbo finishes the story.' Probably about the time of the writing of 'The King of the Golden Hall' he had written (VII.451) that in old age Frodo with Sam had seen Galadriel and Bilbo. On the other hand, in his letter to me of 29 November 1944 (see VIII.219) he was entirely clear – and accurate – in his prevision:

> But the final scene will be the passage of Bilbo and Elrond and Galadriel through the woods of the Shire on their way to the Grey Havens. Frodo will join them and pass over the Sea (linking with the vision he had of a far green country in the house of Tom Bombadil).

Since this is of course the story in the last chapter of *The Lord of the Rings* it is strange indeed to find in the present text that he had departed from it – for 'Frodo rides to the Havens and says farewell to Bilbo' can obviously be interpreted in no other way. I suspect therefore that there is in fact no mystery: that in notes written at great speed my father merely miswrote 'Bilbo' for 'Sam'.

Remarkable also is the reference to the encounter with Saruman – the word *pardoned* here is not certain, but can hardly be read otherwise. That they would meet Saruman again on the homeward journey was an old idea (see 'The Story Foreseen from Moria', VII.212), but then it had taken place at Isengard, and the matter of that scene had of course been removed to a much earlier place in the narrative (VII.436). A later note (VII.287) says that 'Saruman becomes a wandering conjuror and trickster', but nothing further has been told of him since he was left a prisoner in Orthanc guarded by the Ents until now.

VI

THE STEWARD AND THE KING

My remarks about 'The Field of Kormallen' (p. 44) can be repeated of 'The Steward and the King': the preliminary draft ('A') of this chapter, though written roughly and rapidly, was changed very little afterwards. There are nonetheless a number of differences in detail.[1]

A had no title, but 'Faramir and Éowyn' was pencilled in subsequently. A fair copy manuscript 'B' followed, with the chapter-number 'LVI' but no title; to this text the title 'The Watchers on the Walls' was added in pencil, and this was changed to 'The Steward and the King'. In B the page-numbers run only as far as 'And she abode there until King Éomer came' (RK p. 243); at 'All things were now made ready in the City', at the top of a new page, a new numbering from '1' begins.

Of this chapter my father made a third, very fine manuscript 'C', numbering it 'LIV'. Beneath the title 'The Steward and the King' he pencilled '(i) The Steward'; but although there is a large space in the text after 'And she remained there until King Éomer came', where the new page-numbering begins in B, there is no second sub-title.

At the beginning of the chapter in A the Warden of the Houses of Healing, after the words 'He sighed and shook his head' (RK p. 237), continues:

'It may come thus to us all yet,' he said, 'choosing or not choosing. But in the meantime we must endure with patience the hours of waiting. It is not always the easier part. But for you, Lady, you will be the better prepared to face evil that may come in your own manner, if you do as the healers bid, while there is still time.'

This was rejected before the chapter had proceeded much further, for similar words were given to Faramir subsequently in the initial text (RK p. 238). And when the Warden looked out from his window and saw Faramir and Éowyn, finding in the sight a lightening of his care, it is said: 'For it had been reported to him that the Lord Aragorn had said "If she wakes to despair then she will die, unless other healing comes which I cannot give."'

The blue mantle set with stars which Faramir gave to Éowyn when the weather turned cold is in A said to have been made for his mother 'Emmeril', changed in the act of writing to 'Rothinel of Amroth, who died untimely'. This name survived into the following manuscript B, where it was changed to Finduilas (see pp. 58-9).

The words of the Eagle that bore tidings to Minas Tirith of the fall of the Dark Tower were first reported thus:

The realm of Sauron hath ended and the Ring of Doom is no more and the King is victorious, he has passed through the Black Gate in triumph and all his enemies are fled.

The name *Kormallen* entered in this text. My father left a blank for the name as he wrote: 'And Éowyn did not go, though her brother sent word begging her to come to the field of [between Henneth Annûn and Cair Andros]' (cf. RK p. 242 and p. 50 above), but he evidently wrote the name in the margin at once, since it appears in the text as written a few lines later.

In the conversation between Éowyn and Faramir that follows she said, in A, 'I love or have loved another.' This survived in B, where her words were changed to 'I hoped to be loved by another', and then at once to 'I wished'.

Somewhat later in the chapter (RK p. 244) Ioreth (now so spelt; hitherto Yoreth) names the hobbits *Periannath* (cf. *Ernil i Pheriannath* in the chapter 'Minas Tirith', RK p. 41, *Ernil a Pheriannath* VIII.287), and this survived into the First Edition of LR, changed to *Periain* in the Second.

There were substantial differences in the original account of Aragorn's coming to Minas Tirith and his coronation before the walls from the story in RK (pp. 244-6). The entry of Aragorn, Gandalf, Éomer, Imrahil and the four hobbits into the cleared space before the Gateway was very briefly described in A: there was no mention of the Dúnedain nor of Aragorn's apparel. The casket in which the White Crown was laid was not described ('of black *lebethron* bound with silver' B, as in RK; cf. VIII.180). When Faramir, surrendering his office as 'the Last Steward of Gondor', gave Aragorn the white rod Aragorn did not return it to him; he said nothing to Faramir at this point, and Faramir at once proclaimed: 'Men of Gondor, you have no longer a Steward, for behold one has returned to claim the kingship at last. Here is Aragorn son of Arathorn ...' Among Aragorn's titles Faramir names him 'chieftain of the Dúnedain of the North' and does not name him 'bearer of the Star of the North'. After the description of the crown there follows:

And Aragorn knelt, and Faramir upon the one hand and upon the other the Prince Imrahil set the crown upon his head, and then Gandalf laid his hand on Aragorn's shoulder and bade him arise. And when he arose all that beheld him gazed in silence ...

and a light was about him. And then Faramir said 'Behold the King!' and he broke his white rod.

Lastly, when Aragorn came to the Citadel a marginal addition to A says that 'the banner of Tree Crown and Stars was raised above it' ('the banner of the Tree and the Stars' B, as in RK); see VIII.279, 389, 399.

The reference to the Dúnedain 'in silver and grey' and the description of Aragorn's black mail and white mantle clasped with a great green stone was added to B, but the 'star upon his forehead bound by a slender fillet of silver' did not enter until the Second Edition; similarly Faramir still proclaimed him 'chieftain of the Dúnedain of the North' ('of Arnor', Second Edition) and did not name him 'bearer of the Star of the North' in the First Edition (see VIII.299, 309; 389 and note 10).

Rough marginal additions to A make Aragorn return the white rod to Faramir with the words 'That office is not yet wholly at an end' (cf. RK p. 245: 'That office is not ended, and it shall be thine and thy heirs' as long as my line shall last'), and give a first draft of his wish that he should be crowned by those 'by whose labours and valour I have come to my inheritance'. Here the ceremony takes this form: 'Gandalf took the crown and bade Frodo and Sam lay their hands also upon it, and they set the White Crown of Gondor upon the head of Aragorn'; whereas in RK, at Aragorn's request, Frodo brought the crown to Gandalf, who then performed the crowning alone. In B the text of RK was reached at all points in this scene apart from the words of Elendil repeated by Aragorn when he held up the crown,[2] which take the form: *Et Éarello Endorenna lendien. Símane maruvan, ar hildinyar, kenn' Iluve-metta!* A translation pencilled in later is virtually the same as that in RK (p. 246): 'Out of the Great Sea to Middle-earth have I come. Here will I abide, and my heirs, unto the ending of the world.' In the third manuscript C the words remained the same as in B, apart from *tenn'* (as in RK) for *kenn'*, but were subsequently changed to *Et Éarello Endorenna nilendie. Sinome nimaruva yo hildinyar tenn' Ambar-metta!*

A notable visitor to Minas Tirith among the many embassies that came to the King is found in A:

... and the slaves of Mordor he set free and gave them all the lands about Lake Núrnen for their own. And last of all there came to him Ghân-buri-Ghân of the Wild Woods and two of the headmen, and they were clad in garments of green leaves to do honour to the king, and they laid their foreheads on his feet; but he bade them rise up and blessed them and gave them the Forest of Druadan for their own, so that no man should ever enter it without their leave.

This was not rejected on the manuscript, but it is not present in B. For the further history of the last encounter with the Wild Men of the Woods see pp. 61–2, 67–8.

Éowyn's words to Faramir (RK p. 248), saying that she must now return to Rohan with Éomer, but that after the funeral of Théoden she will return, are absent from A (but were added to B). The statements in RK that the Riders of Rohan left Minas Tirith on the eighth of May and that the sons of Elrond went with them are not found in any of the texts, and they remain absent in the First Edition; on the other hand the return of Elladan and Elrohir to Minas Tirith with the company from Rivendell and Lothlórien (RK p. 250) is already found in A. It is told in A that 'the Companions of the Ring lived with Gandalf in a house in the Citadel, and went to and fro as they wished; but Legolas sat most[ly] on the walls and looked south towards the sea.' That the house was in the Citadel was not repeated in B, which retained however the words concerning Legolas; these were lost, possibly unintentionally, in C.

In the story of the ascent of Mindolluin by Gandalf and Aragorn (RK pp. 248–50) there are some differences from the final form to mention. In the original text it is not said that they went up by night and surveyed the lands in the early morning, nor is there mention of the ancient path to the hallow 'where only the kings had been wont to go'; and Gandalf in his words to Aragorn does not speak of the Three Rings, but says:

'... For though much has been saved, much is passing away. And all these lands that you see, and those that lie about, shall be dwellings and realms of Men, whom you must guide. For this is the beginning of the Dominion of Men, and other kindreds will depart, dwindle, and fade.'

B has the final text in all this. In A Aragorn says 'I have still twice the span of other men'; this was retained through the following texts and not changed until the galley proof to the reading of RK (where there is a difference between the First and Second Editions: in the First he says 'I may have life far longer than other men', but in the Second 'I shall').

When Aragorn saw the sapling at the edge of the snow he cried, in A, *En túvien!*, which in B becomes *En a túvien!* This was retained in C but corrected to *En [?in]túviet*; on the final (typescript) text of the chapter this was retained, but then erased and *Yé! utúvienyes* written in its place. The passage continues in A, in extremely difficult handwriting:

'... I have found it, for here is a scion of Nimloth eldest of trees. And how comes it here, for it is not yet itself seven years old?'

And Gandalf said: 'Verily here is a sapling of the line of Telperion Ninquelóte that the Elves of Middle-earth name Nimloth. Nimloth the fair of many names, Silivros and Celeborn[3] and Galathilion of old. But who shall say how it comes here in the hour that is appointed? But the birds of the air are many, and maybe down the ages as lord followed lord . . . . . in the City and the tree withered, here where none looked for it the [?race] of Nimloth has [?flowered already] hidden on the mountain, even as Elendil's race lay hid in the wastes of the North. Yet the line of Nimloth is older far than your line, lord Elessar.'

With the names that appear in this passage cf. the *Quenta Silmarillion* in V.209, §16:

Silpion the one was called in Valinor, and Telperion and Ninquelótë and many names in song beside; but the Gnomes name him Galathilion.

A footnote to the text (V.210) adds:

Other names of Silpion among the Gnomes are Silivros glimmering rain (which in Elvish form is Silmerossë), Nimloth pale blossom, Celeborn tree of silver . . .

B has here the text of RK, in which Aragorn does not name 'the Eldest of Trees', and Gandalf says: 'Verily this is a sapling of the line of Nimloth the fair; and that was a seedling of Galathilion, and that a fruit of Telperion of many names, Eldest of Trees.' In *The Silmarillion* chapter 5 (p. 59) it is told that Yavanna made for the Elves of Tirion

. . . a tree like to a lesser image of Telperion, save that it did not give light of its own being; Galathilion it was named in the Sindarin tongue. This tree was planted in the courts beneath the Mindon and there flourished, and its seedlings were many in Eldamar. Of these one was afterwards planted in Tol Eressëa, and it prospered there, and was named Celeborn; thence came in the fullness of time, as is elsewhere told, Nimloth, the White Tree of Númenor.[4]

In A the sapling did not 'hold only lightly to the earth', but 'Aragorn and Gandalf dug deep.'

In the account of the riding from Rivendell and Lórien at the end of the chapter it is not said in any of the texts that Elrond brought the sceptre of Annúminas and surrendered it to Aragorn; this was only inserted on the final proof. Elrond's daughter is named Finduilas (VIII.370, 386, 425; at this stage Faramir's mother was named Rothinel, p. 54); and in A my father added, after 'Finduilas his daughter', '[and daughter of Celebrian child of Galadriel].' This is the first mention of Celebrian, by this or any name. In the last sentence of the chapter in A Aragorn 'wedded Finduilas Halfelven'; this name survived into B, where Faramir's mother Rothinel was changed to

Finduilas, and Elrond's daughter Finduilas was changed to Arwen, called Undómiel.[5]

NOTES

1   All names in RK not mentioned in my account can be presumed to be present already in A, with the exception of *Beregond*, which was only changed from *Berithil* on manuscript C. Thus Elfhelm is called 'Elfhelm the Marshal' (RK p. 244; cf. VIII.352); and the last king of the line of Anárion is Eärnur, here first named (RK p. 245; cf. VIII.153). The rather puzzling reference to Min-Rimmon (RK p. 245: 'tidings had gone out into all parts of Gondor, from Min-Rimmon even to Pinnath Gelin and the far coasts of the sea') goes back to A.

2   The words of Elendil do not appear in A.

3   In A the name *Celeborn* is spelt with *C*; so also *Celebrian*. In this chapter and in the next the *C* spelling reverted to *K* in the finely-written third manuscripts, but on both it was then corrected back to *C*.

4   Cf. also the *Akallabêth* in *The Silmarillion*, p. 263, and *Of the Rings of Power and the Third Age*, ibid. p. 291.

5   Arwen first emerged in the fair copy of the following chapter, 'Many Partings': see p. 66.

Note on the Chronology

A curious point of chronology that arises in this chapter concerns the lapse of time between the departure of the host from Minas Tirith and the destruction of the Ring.

At the beginning of the chapter, against the words 'When the Captains were but two days gone', the figure '19' is written in the margin of A, i.e. March 19. This is the chronology described in VIII.432, according to which the march from Minas Tirith began on the 17th (the 18th in RK).

When in RK (p. 239) it is said that 'the fifth day came since the Lady Éowyn went first to Faramir', and that was the day of the destruction of the Ring and the fall of the Dark Tower, the same is said in A (and subsequent texts); and at the head of that page my father noted: 'F. sees E. on 19.   20, 21, 22, 23, 24, 25.' This day was therefore the 24th of March. But this is strange, since already in the first draft of 'The Field of Kormallen' Gandalf had declared that 'in Gondor the New Year will always begin on the 25th of March when Sauron fell ...' (p. 46). In A, Éowyn says that this day was 'seven days since [Aragorn] rode away' (RK p. 240), which agrees with the date of March 24 for the destruction of the Ring. But my father changed 'seven', as he wrote, to 'nine', which would presumably give March 26 as the day of deliverance. He then changed 'nine' to 'eight', giving the

25th as the day, and 'eight' is the reading in B and C, changed in C to 'seven' as in RK: this presumably implies that the date of the departure from Minas Tirith had been changed to the 18th. – On the significance of the date 25 March see T. A. Shippey, *The Road to Middle-Earth* (1982) pp. 151–2.

VII

MANY PARTINGS

The original draft of this chapter ('A') was paginated continuously with that of 'The Steward and the King' and bore no title. In comparison with its subsequent form my father's initial account of the 'many partings' was remarkably brief and spare; and though his handwriting is very difficult and here and there altogether illegible I shall give a substantial part of it in full, for it differs in very many points from the story in RK.

The opening, however, remained almost unchanged from first draft to final text (apart from *Queen Finduilas* for *Queen Arwen*), as far as ' "Then I beg leave to depart soon," said Frodo.' Then follows (with no mention of the Queen's gift):

'In three days we will go,' said Aragorn. 'For we shall ride with you great part of the way. We too have errands to do.'
  And so it was that the King of Gondor and his Queen set out once more upon the North Roads, and many knights rode with them; and the Princes of Dol Amroth and of Ithilien; and King Éomer and his householdmen were also in that riding, for he had come to the wedding of his lord and brother. And with slow songs of the Mark they brought from the Halls [*probably for* Hallows] and his resting in Rath Dínen King Théoden upon a golden bier; and as one that still slept deeply they laid him upon a great wain with Riders of Rohan all about it, and his banner borne before. And Merry being his esquire, and a Knight of the Riddermark, rode upon the wain and kept the arms of the dead king. But for the other companions steeds were furnished according to their stature, and Frodo and Sam rode at the king's side with Gandalf upon Shadowfax; and with them also went Legolas and Gimli upon Hasufel[1] who had borne them so far.[2]
  And slowly and at peace they passed into Anórien. And .... the Greywood[3] under Amon Dîn.

Here my father stopped and asked whether the homage of the Wild Men should be put here – referring, presumably, to the story in the original text of 'The Steward and the King', where Ghân-buri-Ghân and two of his headmen actually came to Minas Tirith (p. 56). He then wrote: 'and there stood Ghân-buri-Ghân by the eaves of the trees, and did them homage as they passed' (see p. 67). The text continues:

And so at last after many days (15?) they brought King Théoden back to his own land, and they came to Edoras, and there they stayed and rested; and never so fair and full of light was the Golden Hall, for no king of the City of the South had ever come thither before. And there they held the funeral of Théoden, and he was laid in a house of stone with many fair things, and over him was raised a great mound, the eighth of those upon the east side of the Barrowfields, and it was covered with green turves of grass [and] of fair Evermind. And then the Riders of the King's House rode about it, and one among them sang a song of Théoden Thengel's son that brought light to the eyes of the folk of the Mark and stirred the hearts of all, even those that knew not [that] speech. And Merry who stood at the foot of the mound wept.[4]

And when the burial was over and the last song was ended there was a great feast in the hall, and when they came to the time when all should drink to the memories of mighty men forth came Éowyn Lady of Rohan, golden as the sun and white as snow, and she brought forth the cup to Éomer King of the Mark, and he drank to the memory of Théoden. And then a minstrel sang naming all the kings of the [?Mark] in their order, and last King Éomer; and Aragorn arose and [?wished him] hail [and] drank to him. And then Gandalf arose and bid all men rise, and they rose, and he said: 'Here is a last hail[5] ere the feast endeth. Last but not least. For I name now [one >] those who shall not be forgotten and without whose valour nought else that was done would have availed; and I name before you all Frodo of the Shire and Samwise his servant. And the bards and the minstrels should give them new names: *Bronwe athan Harthad* and *Harthad Uluithiad*, Endurance beyond Hope and Hope unquenchable.'[6]

And to those names men drank in honour; but Sam went very red, and murmured to Frodo: 'I don't know what my Dad would think of the change: he was always against outlandish names. "The gentry can do as they please," he said, "with their Roriuses and Ronshuses, but for plain folk something shorter wears better." But even if I could say the name, I think it don't suit. My hope ... . low, Mr. Frodo, ...'[7]

The announcement by Éomer of the betrothal of Faramir and

Éowyn and the words of Éowyn with Aragorn are particularly hard to read, but the passage does not differ significantly from that in RK (pp. 255–6). The text then continues:

And after the feast those that were to go took leave of King Éomer, and Faramir abode with him, for he would not be far from Éowyn any longer. And Finduilas also remained and took leave of her father and brethren. But Aragorn rode on with the companions, and they passed on to Helm's Deep and there rested. And then Legolas repaid his vow to Gimli and went into the Glittering Caves; and when he returned he was silent, for he said that only Gimli could find fit words. 'And now,' said he, 'we will go to Fangorn', at which Gimli looked little pleased.

And so they passed .... to Isengard and saw how the Ents had busied themselves, for all the stone circle was removed and was planted with trees, but in the midst of the orchards Orthanc rose up still, tall and [? unapproachable]. And there was Treebeard and other Ents to welcome them, and he praised all their deeds, of which it seemed he had full tidings. 'But Ents played their part,' said he. 'And there would have been no Golden Hall to return to but for Treebeard and his folk. For we caught a great army of those – *burarum* – those orcs that were coming down through the Wold and we drove them away. Or otherwise the king of the grassland would [?have never] ridden far.'

And Gandalf praised his work, and at last he said farewell with many long words, saying that he had added some new lines. And when Merry and Pippin at last said farewell he .... them and said 'Well, my merry folk! Take a draught before you go!' And they said 'Yes, indeed!' And he looked at them over the bowl, and he said 'Take care! For you have already grown since I saw you!' And they laughed, and then he [?went] sad, and he said 'And don't forget that if you ever hear news of the Entwives you must send word to us.' And Aragorn said 'The East lands now lie open.' But Treebeard shook his head and said that it was far away.

But Legolas and Gimli here said goodbye, and went into Fangorn, and from there they purposed [? to journey] together to their own countries. 'Alas, that our lands lie so far apart! But we will send word to Rivendell.' And Elrond looked at them and said: 'Send rather to the Shire.'

Then they rode to the Gap of Rohan, and Aragorn took leave of them in that very place where Pippin had looked in the Palantír. And Pippin said 'I wish we could have one to see all our friends.' 'But one only now remains,' said Aragorn ....., 'and the king must keep that. But forget not that my realm lies now also in the North; and later on I may come again.'

And so slowly they passed in[to] the waste lands west of the mountains and fared north, and summer wore away; and Galadriel and Celeborn and their folk passed over the Dimrill Stair and went back to Lórien. But Elrond and Gandalf and the hobbits came back at last to Rivendell.

The chapter ends in this earliest form with very rough sketching of the time that the hobbits spent with Bilbo, but most of the essentials of the final form are present. The chief difference lies in Bilbo's gifts: 'Then Bilbo gave Frodo his coat and sword, and he gave Sam a lot of books of lore, and he gave Merry and Pippin a lot of good advice.' Bilbo's verse (*The Road goes ever on and on*) is lacking, but that there should be a verse at this point is indicated on the manuscript. Gandalf's intimation that he would go with the hobbits 'at least as far as Bree' is lacking; and at the departure from Rivendell Elrond's words of farewell to Frodo, though the same as in RK (suggesting that 'about this time of the year' he should 'look for Bilbo in the woods of the Shire'), were heard also by the others: 'And they did not fully understand what he meant, and Gandalf of course would not explain.' The text then runs straight on into what would become the opening of the next chapter, 'Homeward Bound'.

This first manuscript was greatly enlarged by the insertion of new material. The story of the visit to Isengard was elaborated, and Treebeard's account of the release of Saruman from Orthanc now enters – the necessary prelude, of course, to the encounter with Saruman and Wormtongue on the northward journey of the remaining company. There are a number of differences from the text of RK, but they are minor.[8] The farewell speeches of Treebeard with Celeborn and Galadriel now appear, differing from the final form only in the Quenya phrase: *O vanimar vanimalion ontari* (see note 16).

A long rider takes up at the words 'Then they rode towards the Gap of Rohan' (cf. RK p. 260), and the departure of Aragorn is told in almost the same words as in RK; but Galadriel said to him: 'Elfstone, through darkness you have come to your desire. Use well the days of light', and Celeborn said: 'Kinsman, farewell, but your doom is like to mine; for our treasure shall outlast us both' (see pp. 124–5 and note 16).

The story of the meeting with Saruman, which had been very obliquely referred to in 'The Story Foreseen from Kormallen' ('They come on Saruman and he is [?pardoned]', p. 52), was now fully told, but with a number of differences, one very notable. No indication is given of where or when the encounter took place: after the company had crossed the Isen they 'passed into the waste land west of the mountains, and they turned north, and summer wore away. And many days afterward they overtook an old man leaning on a staff ...' See further p. 69.

To Saruman's remark 'I am seeking a way out of his realm' Gandalf at first replies:

'Then you are going the wrong way [*bracketed:* as seems to be your doom], unless you wish to pass into the utter North and there freeze to death. For from the Sea in the West to Anduin and thence many days' march east is the realm of the King, and east ere long it will spread beyond the water of Rúnaeluin.'⁹

Without striking this out my father replaced it by:

'Then you have far to go,' said Gandalf, 'and should be going eastward. Yet even so you would have to travel far, and find the border of his realm ever marching up behind you.'

This was struck through, and the final text here is: ' "Then you have far to go," said Gandalf, "and I see no hope in your journey...." ' Wormtongue still names himself *Frána*, not *Gríma* (cf. VII.445, VIII.55). Most curious is my father's remarkably different initial conception of Saruman's response to Merry's generosity (the sentence that I have bracketed was presumably rejected):

'Mine, mine, yes, and dearly paid for,' said Saruman, clutching at the pouch. And then suddenly he seemed touched. 'Well, I thank you,' he said. '[You do not crow, and your kind looks maybe are not feigned.] You seem an honest fellow, and maybe you did not come to crow over me. I'll tell you something. When you come to the Shire beware of Cosimo, and make haste, or you may go short of leaf.'

'Thankyou,' said Merry, 'and if you get tired of wandering in the wild come to the Shire.'

My father knew that Saruman acquired his supply of pipe-weed from the Shire (see VIII.59, note 8). There is no certain indication that he had at this stage begun to conceive of any more far-reaching relations between Saruman and Cosimo Sackville-Baggins, but in the original draft of 'The Scouring of the Shire' this idea was very fully present (see p. 84). On the other hand, it is a very notable feature of that draft that Saruman was *not* present in person in the Shire and did not preside over the last stages of its spoliation.

Since as will be seen subsequently the whole of the conclusion of *The Lord of the Rings* from 'Many Partings' to the 'Epilogue' was written in one continuous draft, it seems perfectly possible that all this new material was introduced into the original draft of 'Many Partings' *after* the first draft of 'The Scouring of the Shire' had been written. If this is so, it was very probably when writing and developing the present passage that my father first conceived of Saruman's visit to the Shire (as in the story itself the decision to do so also arose in Saruman's mind at this juncture, RK p. 298); possibly it was in fact Merry's extraordinarily artless invitation (though immediately abandoned, as will be seen in a moment) that was the germ of the story.

Precisely what my father had in mind when he wrote Saruman's words here, 'When you come to the Shire beware of Cosimo, and make haste, or you may go short of leaf', I do not know. It certainly shows that Saruman knew what was going on there, but equally certainly it was intended to be taken as good advice on Saruman's part to repay Merry for his gift. But my father marked Merry's reply with a large query, and at once, on the same page, recognising that the pride, bitterness and malevolence of Saruman could never be pierced by such a gesture on the part of Merry Brandybuck, he wrote the passage that stands in RK (p. 262): 'This is but a repayment in token. You took more, I'll be bound ...'

The first draft A was followed by a much-needed fair copy 'B', and that (as in 'The Steward and the King') by a third text 'C' in my father's most handsome script. B was subsequently given the number and title 'LVII Many Partings'.[10] While the final form of the chapter was very largely achieved in B, there remain a number of minor differences from the text of RK; I mention here some of the more noteworthy, and collect a few further details in note 16.

It was in B that the name *Arwen* at last emerged. In the opening paragraph of the chapter in this text the Queen was named *Ellonel*, but this was at once changed back to *Finduilas*, and she is *Finduilas* at the two following occurrences (and *Evenstar* in 'But wear this now in memory of Elfstone and Evenstar with whom your life has been woven,' RK p. 253). It must have been at this point that my father determined that her name was not *Finduilas*, and that he must find out what it was; for on a page of rough drafting for sentences in the opening of the chapter he is seen experimenting with other names, as *Amareth, Emrahil.* He wrote *Elrond Elladan Elrohir Emrahil, Finduilas* > *Emrahil*, and beside this (evidently to avoid the clash with *Imrahil*) *Imrahil* > *Ildramir*; but then, clearly and firmly, *Arwen Undómiel.* Immediately after this in text B as written Éomer says to Gimli 'But now I will put Queen Arwen Evenstar first' (RK p. 253).

In a first form of Arwen's words to Frodo she says: 'Mine is the choice of Lúthien, and I have chosen as she at last', the words 'at last' being omitted in a second version of the passage; and of her gift to him she says in B:

'... But in my stead you shall go, Ringbearer, when the time comes, and if you then desire it: for your wounds have been grievous and your burden heavy. But you shall pass into the West until all your wounds and weariness are healed. [*Struck out at once:* Take this token and Elrond will not refuse you.' And she took from her hair a white gem like a star] Take with you the Phial of Galadriel and Círdan will not refuse you. But wear this now in memory of Elfstone and Evenstar with whom your life has been woven!' And she took a white gem . . .

In the third manuscript C the text of RK was reached.

Merethrond, the Great Hall of Feasts in Minas Tirith (RK p. 253) is said in B to be 'in the Citadel' (a statement omitted in C). On a page of rough drafting for this passage my father dashed off a little plan of the Citadel. This is shown as a circle with seven small circles (towers) at equal distances within the circumference, one of these standing beside the entrance. Beyond the Court of the Fountain is marked, at the centre, the White Tower and Hall of the Kings, and beyond that again, on the west side of the Citadel, the King's House. To the right (north) of the White Tower is the Hall of Feasts. The outlines of other buildings are roughed in between the towers.

When Aragorn and Éomer came to the Hallows 'they came to the tomb that had been built in Rath Dínen' (where C has the reading of RK, 'the tombs in Rath Dínen'); and returning with the bier they 'passed through the City, where all the people stood in silence; but the knights of Rohan that followed the bier sang in their own tongue a lament for the fallen' (so in A, p. 61, 'with slow songs of the Mark'). This was changed to 'the knights of Rohan . . . walked also in silence, for the time for song was not yet come' (cf. RK p. 253).

The encounter with Ghân-buri-Ghân (see pp. 61–2) was further developed, re-using the original passage in the previous chapter (p. 56) where Ghân-buri-Ghân came to Minas Tirith:

. . . and they came to the Grey Wood under Amon Dín. And there beside the road in the shadow of the trees stood Ghân of the Wild Woods and two of his headmen beside him, and they were clad all in garments of green leaves to do honour to the king. For Ghân-buri-Ghân said: 'He was great king; he drove away dark with bright iron. And now men of Stonehouses have king, he will not let dark come back.' And he and his headmen laid their foreheads upon Aragorn's feet; and he bade them rise up, and he blessed them, and gave them the Forest of Druadan to be their own, so that no man should ever enter it without their leave. Then they bowed and vanished into the trees.

This was struck through, and a version replacing it is found written on the last page of text B of 'The Steward and the King', almost as in

RK (p. 254), in which the Wild Men remain invisible and only their drums are heard. In this version the heralds added: 'and whoso slays one of his people slays the king's friends.'

All the names of the Kings of the Mark, recited by the minstrel in the Golden Hall, are now given, but my father missed out *Folcwine*, great-grandfather of Théoden: this was a mere slip, since Folcwine appears in the earliest list of the kings (VIII.408), and without him there are only seven mounds on the east side of the Barrowfield. But the omission escaped notice, and Folcwine was not inserted until the Second Edition. The eleventh king (*Háma* in the original list) now becomes *Léof* (changed to *Léofa* in the Second Edition).[11]

In the parting of Merry from Éomer and Éowyn (RK p. 256) they address him as 'Meriadoc of the Shire and of the Mark' – the name *Holdwine* ('of the Mark') was only introduced on the galley proof; and Éomer says this of the gift of the horn, which he does not attribute to Éowyn:

'... but you will take naught but the arms that were given to you. This I suffer, because though we are of other lands and kind, still you are to me a dear kinsman whose love can only be requited with love. But this one gift I beg you now to take ...'

The horn is described in the same words as in RK; but then follows:

'This is an heirloom of our house,' said Éowyn, 'and in the deeps of time it was made for our forefathers by the dwarves [*struck out:* of Dale], and Eorl the Young brought it from the North.'

The statement that the horn 'came from the hoard of Scatha the Worm' entered on the galley proof.

The meeting with Treebeard reaches in this text B the form in RK at almost all points. Treebeard's denunciation of the Orcs runs here: *henulka-morimaite-quingatelko-tingahondo-rakkalepta-saurikumba*.[12] A curious point is that Gandalf says here 'The Third Age begins', which was repeated in C but there emended to 'The New Age begins' as in RK. With this may be compared my father's letter of November 1944 (*Letters* no. 91, also VIII.219): 'So ends the Middle Age and the Dominion of Men begins', and, further back, Saruman's speech to Gandalf in Isengard (VII.150): 'The Elder Days are gone. The Middle Days are passing. The Younger Days are beginning'; but in 'The Story Foreseen from Kormallen' (p. 52) is found 'The end of the Third Age is presaged' and 'End of the Third Age'.

Gandalf's response to Treebeard's report that he had allowed Saruman to go free remains as it was in A (see note 8): Treebeard now says 'A snake without fangs may crawl where he will', but this does not yet prompt Gandalf to the observation that Saruman 'had still one tooth left ... the poison of his voice', which entered in C. Gimli, in his farewell, still concludes as in A (p. 63): 'Alas! that our lands lie so far apart. But we will send word to Rivendell when we may'; to which Elrond now replies: 'Send rather to Gondor, or else to the Shire!'

Again as in A (note 8), Treebeard does not say when the release of Saruman had taken place, and this remained into the First Edition; in the Second Edition 'Yes, he is gone' was changed to 'Yes, he is gone seven days.'[13]

The actual encounter with Saruman now differed virtually not at all from RK, but the placing of it was somewhat different in the First Edition from the revised version in the Second. The text of the First Edition ran thus (RK pp. 260–1):

Soon the dwindling company came to the Isen, and crossed over it, and came into the waste lands beyond, and then they turned northwards, and passed by the borders of Dunland. And the Dunlendings fled and hid themselves, for they were afraid of Elvish folk, though few indeed ever came to their country. But the travellers did not heed them, for they were still a great company and were well provided with all that they needed; and they went on their way at their leisure, setting up tents when they would; and as they went the summer wore away.

After they had passed by Dunland and were come to places where few folk dwelt, and even birds and beasts were seldom to be seen, they journeyed through a wood climbing down from the hills at the feet of the Misty Mountains that now marched on their right hand. As they came out again into open country they overtook an old man leaning on a staff ...

As noted above, in the Second Edition Treebeard told Gandalf that Saruman had been gone seven days; and in the revision of the passage just cited the First Edition text 'After they had passed by Dunland and were come to places where few folk dwelt, and even birds and beasts were seldom to be seen, they journeyed through a wood ...' was altered to 'On the sixth day since their parting from the King they journeyed through a wood ...' By this change the company was still in Dunland when they came upon Saruman, and a little later in the narrative, after 'I fancy he could do some mischief still in a small mean way' (RK p. 263), my father added in the Second Edition: 'Next day they went on into northern Dunland, where no men now dwelt, though it was a green and pleasant country' (northern Dunland, rather than the country north of Dunland, now becoming the uninhabited region).

From this point, the end of the Saruman episode, the text B continues:

September came in with a golden morning shimmering above

silver mists; and looking out they saw away to the east the sun catching three peaks that thrust up through floating cloud into the sky: Caradhras, Celebras, and Fanuiras.[14] They were near once more to the Gates of Moria. And now came another parting...

This must mean that it was on the first of September that they saw the Mountains of Moria. This was developed by a late emendation to C to the reading of the First Edition:

September came in with golden days and silver nights. At last a fair morning dawned, shimmering above gleaming mists; and looking from their camp on a low hill the travellers saw away in the east the Sun catching three peaks that thrust up into the sky through floating clouds: Caradhras, Celebdil, and Fanuidhol. They were near to the Gates of Moria.

Here now for seven days they tarried, for the time was at hand for another parting...

In the Second Edition this passage (from 'September came in ...') was extended by references to the Swanfleet river, the falls, and the ford by which the company crossed.[15]

In various small points B received further alteration in the story of the sojourn of the hobbits in Rivendell, but effectively the final form was now reached.[16]

NOTES

1 *Hasufel* was presumably no more than a slip of memory, though it survived until emended on the third manuscript. Hasufel was Aragorn's horse of Rohan, and the horse that carried Legolas and Gimli was Arod.

2 Pippin is not mentioned, but in a rejected form of the passage it is said that he 'rode with the Prince of Ithilien, for he was the esquire of the Steward.'

3 *the Greywood*: previously named ('Grey Woods') only on a small map in a draft text of 'The Ride of the Rohirrim', VIII.353.

4 Here there is a mark of insertion, probably referring to verses that would be given at this point (although there are no verses here in the second and third manuscripts: see note 16).

5 In *wished him hail* (if correctly read) in the preceding sentence *hail* means 'health, happiness, welfare'; in Gandalf's *Here is a last hail* the word seems to be used elliptically, as if 'Here is a last drinking (of) hail'.

6 The word that I give as *athan* is very unclear and uncertain.

7 Gandalf's praise of Frodo and Sam, and this engaging glimpse of

the Gaffer amid the ceremoniousness of Edoras, had disappeared in the second text. *Ronshus* is evidently his clipped form of *Gerontius*, the name of the Old Took; and I suppose that he attached the 'learned' or high-falutin ending *-us* to Rory (Brandybuck). But the Gaffer's views were not entirely lost. When discussing with Frodo the name of his eldest child ('The Grey Havens', RK p. 306) Sam said: 'I've heard some beautiful names on my travels, but I suppose they're a bit too grand for daily wear and tear, as you might say. The Gaffer, he says: "Make it short, and then you won't have to cut it short before you can use it." ' — Sam's final remark is unfortunately altogether illegible; the word preceding *low* might possibly be *getting*, or *pretty*, but the word preceding that is certainly not *was*.

8 The two sentinel trees that grew now where the gates of Isengard had stood do not appear. The words of Aragorn and Gandalf with Treebeard after his mention of the destruction of the Orcs (whom he apostrophises only in English adjectives) in the Wold were different from those in RK (p. 258), though a part of this dialogue was used a little later in the final text:

> 'We know it,' said Aragorn, 'and never shall it be forgotten, nor your storming of Isengard, and it is our hope that your forest may grow again in peace. There is room and to spare west of the mountains.'
> 'Forest may grow,' said Treebeard sadly; 'woods may spread, but not Ents; there are no Entings now.'
> 'Never at least while the Mark and Gondor remain,' said Gandalf; 'and that will have to be very long indeed to seem long to Ents. But what of your most important task, Fangorn? . . .'

Treebeard does not say how long it was since Saruman had gone (see p. 69); and Gandalf does not tell him that Saruman had found his soft spot and persuaded him by 'the poison of his voice', but says merely 'Well, he's gone then, and that is all there is to be said' (reminiscent of his resigned 'Well, well, he is gone' when he heard from Legolas at the Council of Elrond of Gollum's escape, FR p. 269). Quickbeam does not appear in the handing over of the keys to Orthanc: ' "It is locked," said Treebeard, "locked by Saruman, and here are the keys," and he gave three black keys to Aragorn.'

9 *Rúnaeluin*: the last four letters are not perfectly clear, but this seems much the most probable interpretation. Can *Rúnaeluin* be the Sea of Rhûn?

10 The third manuscript C was given the chapter-number 'LV'. This reduction of the numbers by two begins with 'The Tower of Kirith Ungol' (p. 25).

11   In the First Edition, while the eleventh king is named *Léof* by the minstrel in Edoras in 'Many Partings', in the list of the Kings of the Mark in Appendix A (II) the eleventh king is *Brytta*, with no explanation given. In the Second Edition the explanation was added: 'He was called by his people *Léofa*, for he was loved by all; he was openhanded and a help to all the needy.'

12   The English adjectives in B are the same as those in RK: 'evileyed, blackhanded, bowlegged, flinthearted, clawfingered, foulbellied, bloodthirsty'. In C the words *quingatelko* and *rakkalepta* were omitted, and then *henulka* and *saurikumba* were struck out and *tingahondo* changed to *sincahondo*. Finally *sincahondo* was changed on the printer's typescript to *sincahonda* as in RK.

13   On a copy of the First Edition that my father used to make alterations for incorporation in the Second Edition he added to the section 'The Chief Days from the Fall of the Barad-dûr to the End of the Third Age' in Appendix B the entry '*August 15*   Treebeard releases Saruman', but this was not for some reason included in the Second Edition. See the Note on Chronology below.

14   On the names *Celebras* and *Fanuiras* see VII.174, 306.

15   The course of this river was marked already on the First Map (VII.305), flowing down from the Misty Mountains to join the Greyflood above Tharbad. It was not referred to in the text of the First Edition, but was named the *Glanduin* in Appendix A (I, iii, first paragraph). The accidents or misunderstandings that bedevilled its representation on the map accompanying *The Lord of the Rings* are detailed in *Unfinished Tales* pp. 263–5.

16   It is not said in B that the only part of the hobbits' story that really interested Bilbo was the account of the crowning and marriage of Aragorn; nor that he had forgotten that he had already given Sting and the mithril-coat to Frodo; nor that his books of lore had red backs. All these changes entered in the third manuscript C. The books were labelled *Translations from the Elvish, by B. B. Esquire*; *Esquire* was removed on the galley proof.

   I record here various other details, mostly concerning names, in which B differed from RK.

   The reference to Merry as 'a Knight of the Riddermark' was retained from A (p. 61) and then struck out. On *Hasufel* for *Arod* see note 1.

   The alliterative verses of the song of the Riders of Rohan as they rode round Théoden's barrow were only introduced on a rider to the fourth text, the typescript for the printer, together with the passage preceding them in which the song of the Riders brought to mind 'the voice of Eorl crying above the battle upon the Field of Celebrant', and 'the horn of Helm was loud in the mountains'. The king's minstrel, who made the song, was

Gleowin in B, *Gléowine* in C; and *the Barrowfields* of A become *the Barrowfield* in B.

In Éomer's farewell words to Merry (RK p. 256) he speaks of his deeds 'upon the fields of Mundberg', emended on C to *Mundburg* (see VIII.355–6).

Treebeard's name of Lórien was spelt *Laurelindórinan*, and this survived into the First Edition, becoming *Laurelindórenan* in the Second. He still says to Galadriel and Celeborn *O vanimar vanimalion ontari* (p. 64), *O* being changed to *A* on text B and *ontari* to *nostari* on C. The comma after *vanimar* was added in the Second Edition. In VIII.20 I mentioned late notes of my father's on the fragments of other languages found in *The Lord of the Rings*, which for the greater part of the book are so hastily written as to be mostly unusable. His translation of *O vanimar, vanimálion nostari* can however be made out (in the light of the Quenya words themselves): 'fair ones begetters of fair ones', and with this is a note '*nosta* beget'; cf. the *Etymologies* in Vol.V, stems BAN, NŌ, ONO.

Wormtongue's name remained *Frána* (p. 65) in B and C, but was changed to *Gríma* on the final typescript; and Gandalf still calls Butterbur *Barnabas* (RK p. 265).

Note on the Chronology

In the original draft A of this chapter there were scarcely any indications of chronology: Aragorn tells Frodo (p. 61) that they will depart from Minas Tirith in three days' time, but this only relates to the end of 'the days of rejoicing', of indeterminate length; and it was fifteen days' journey from Minas Tirith to Rohan.

In B Aragorn tells Frodo that they will leave in seven days, and that 'in three days now Éomer will return hither to bear Théoden back to rest in the Mark', as he duly did; and all this is retained in *The Lord of the Rings*, together with the fifteen days of the journey to Rohan. But neither B nor C give much more indication than did the original draft of the time taken over the stages of the journey from Edoras to Rivendell, and it may be that my father did not attend to the matter closely until the final preparation of the book. It is a curious fact that the chronology of 'The Chief Days from the Fall of the Barad-dûr to the End of the Third Age' in Appendix B (and which is the same in this respect in both editions) does not agree with the text of 'Many Partings' in respect either of Éomer's return in relation to the setting out for Edoras or of the time taken on that journey. In the chronology of 'The Chief Days' Éomer returned to Minas Tirith on July 18, and the riding from the City with King Théoden's wain took place on the following day, July 19, not four days later as in 'Many Partings'; while the arrival at Edoras is dated August 7, eighteen days later, not fifteen as in the text.

As I have noted already, no indication of date was given for the meeting of Saruman with the travellers as they rode north even in the First Edition; in the Second Edition the passage was altered to say that the meeting took place on the sixth day since they parted from the King, and they were still in Dunland (see p. 69). But in fact this dating was already present in the First Edition, in the chronology of 'The Chief Days' in *The Tale of Years*:

August 22 They come to Isengard; they take leave of the King of the West at sunset.

August 28 They overtake Saruman; Saruman turns towards the Shire.

As the third text C was written it was still on September 1 that the travellers saw the Mountains of Moria, but late emendation (see p. 70) produced, or satisfied, the chronology of 'The Chief Days':

September 6 They halt in sight of the Mountains of Moria.

September 13 Celeborn and Galadriel depart, the others set out for Rivendell.

On September 21, the day before Bilbo's birthday, Gandalf and the hobbits returned to Rivendell, having taken (being mounted) a much shorter time than they took to reach Moria on their outward journey, nine months before.

VIII

HOMEWARD BOUND

The original draft A of 'Many Partings' continued on into the opening of 'Homeward Bound' (see p. 64), but my father drew a line of separation, and began a new pagination, probably at an early stage. At the same time he scribbled in a title for the new chapter: 'Homecoming'. This text runs on with continuous pagination right through to the end of *The Lord of the Rings*, and included the Epilogue.

This last of the first drafts ends the work in style: if not the most difficult of all the manuscripts of *The Lord of the Rings* it certainly has few rivals. As far as the Battle of Bywater (see p. 93) it gives the impression of having been written in one long burst, and with increasing rapidity. Ideas that appear in earlier reaches of the text are contradicted later without correction of the former passages. In the part of it that corresponds to 'Homeward Bound' and the beginning of 'The Scouring of the Shire', however, the text does not present excessive difficulty, chiefly because the final form of the story was not very substantially changed from that in the original draft, but also because my father's handwriting, while very rough throughout, declined only gradually as the text proceeded.

I break the text here into three chapters as in RK. Throughout, the original draft is of course called 'A'. Of the tale of the visit to *The Prancing Pony* there is not a great deal to record. It opens thus (RK p. 268):

So now they turned their faces for home; and though they rode now they rode but slowly. But they were at peace and in no haste, and if they missed their companions of their adventures, still they had Gandalf, and the journey went well enough when once they passed beyond Weathertop. For at the Fords of Bruinen Frodo halted and was loth to ride through, and from here on to Weathertop he was silent and ill at ease; but Gandalf said nothing.

And when they came to the hill he said 'Let us hasten', and would not look towards it. 'My wound aches,' he said, 'and the memory of darkness is heavy on me. Are there not things, Gandalf, that cannot ever be wholly healed?'

'Alas, it is so,' said Gandalf.

'It is so I guess with my wounds,' said Frodo. ...

This page of A (carrying the end of the later 'Many Partings' and the beginning of 'Homeward Bound') was replaced, in all probability very soon, by a new page with a chapter number, 'LVIII', and in this the opening passage draws nearer to that in RK: the date of the crossing of the Fords of Bruinen is given (the sixth of October, as in RK), and Frodo speaks of his pain there, not below Weathertop; but he says: 'It's my shoulder, my wound aches. And my finger too, the one that is gone, but I feel pain in it, and the memory of darkness is heavy on me.'[1]

When Butterbur came to the door of *The Prancing Pony* he did not, as in RK, misunderstand Nob's cry 'They've come back' and come rushing out armed with a club:

And out came Barnabas wiping his hand on his apron and looking as bustled as ever, though there seemed few folk about, and not much talk in the Common Room; indeed he looked in the dim lamplight rather more wrinkled and careworn.

'Well, well,' he said, 'I never expected to see any of you folk again and that's a fact: going off into the wild with that Trotter . . .'

Whatever response Butterbur made to Gandalf's request 'And if you have any tobacco we'll bless you. Ours has long since been finished' is not reported. When Butterbur objects (RK p. 272) that he doesn't want 'a whole crowd of strangers settling here and camping there and tearing up the wild country' Gandalf tells him:

'. . . There's room enough for realms between Isen and Greyflood, and along the shores between Greyflood and Brandy-wine. And many folk used to dwell north away, a hundred miles and more from you, on the North Down[s] and by Nenuial or Evendimmer, if you have heard of it. I should not wonder if the Deadmen's Dike is filled with living men again. Kings' Norbury is its right name in your tongue. One day the King may come again.'[2]

Apart from these passages the text of 'Homeward Bound' in RK was virtually present in the draft text,[3] though naturally with many small changes in the dialogue still to come, until the end of the chapter: here there is a notable difference in the story. The conversation of the hobbits as they left Bree is much as in RK, but without Merry's reference to pipe-weed and without Gandalf's reference to Saruman and his interest in the Shire:

'I wonder what he [Butterbur] means,' said Frodo.

'I can guess some of it at any rate,' said Sam gloomily. 'What I saw in the Mirror. Trees cut down and all, and the old gaffer turned out. I ought to have turned back sooner.'

'Whatever it is it'll be that Cosimo at the bottom of it,' said Pippin.

'Deep but not at the bottom,' said Gandalf.

This stands near but not at the foot of a page. Across the empty space my father wrote this note:

Gandalf should stay at Bree. He should say: 'You may find trouble, but I want you to settle it yourselves. Wizards should not interfere in such things. Don't crack nuts with a sledge-hammer, or you'll crack the kernels. And many times over anyway. I'll be along some time.'

The empty space had perhaps been intended to mark a pause; at any rate this note was written in later (though not much later), since the text continues on the following page and Gandalf has not left the hobbits: he is present at and plays a part in the encounter with the gate-guards on the Brandywine Bridge (at the beginning of the next chapter in RK, 'The Scouring of the Shire': pp. 79–80).

They passed the point on the East Road where they had taken leave of Bombadil, and half they expected to see him standing there to greet them as they went by. But there was no sign of him, and there was a grey mist over the Barrow-down[s] southward and a deep veil hid the Old Forest far away.

Frodo halted and looked wistfully south. 'I should like to see the old fellow again. I wonder how he's getting on.'

'As well as ever, you may be sure,' said Gandalf. 'Quite untroubled, and if I may say so not at all interested in anything that has happened to us. There will be time later to visit him. If I were you I should press on for home now, or we'll not come to Brandywine Bridge till the gates are locked.'

'But there aren't any gates,' said Merry, 'at least not on the Road. There's the Buckland Gate of course.'

'There weren't any gates, you mean,' said Gandalf. 'I think you'll find some now.'

They did. It was long after dark when tired and wet they came to the Brandywine and found the way barred at both ends of the Bridge ...

The first draft was followed by a fair copy ('B') of 'Homeward Bound' with that title, and then by a fine and elegant manuscript ('C').

Already in B the final form of the chapter was achieved at almost every point.[4]

NOTES

1 The reason for the change was that the recurrence of the pain of Frodo's wound should depend on the date, not on the place. See further p. 112, notes 3 and 4.

2 The name *Nenuial* first occurs here. The curious (but certain) form *Evendimmer* I cannot explain; *Evendim* (and *Fornost Erain*) appear in the second text of the chapter.

3 The return of Bill the Pony is recorded by Butterbur in almost the same words as in RK (cf. VII.448, VIII.219). – Two other minor points may be mentioned here. Gandalf's sword (RK p. 272) is called *Orcrist* (the name of the sword of Thorin Oakenshield): this was a mere slip, which however survived into the third manuscript of the chapter, where it was changed to *Glamdring*. The entrance into Bree by the road from Weathertop was called 'the East-gate', and only changed to 'the South-gate' on the typescript for the printer; cf. the plan of Bree, VI.335.

4 In his parting words to the hobbits Gandalf says in B: 'I am not coming to the Shire. You must settle its affairs yourselves. To bring me in would be using a sledgehammer to crack nuts.' With the last sentence cf. the note, written on text A, given on p. 77. – *Trotter* and *Cosimo* survived into the third manuscript C and were only then changed to *Strider* and *Lotho*; *Barnabas* survived into the final typescript and was corrected on that to *Barliman*.

IX

THE SCOURING OF THE SHIRE

As has been seen in the last chapter, the long draft text A moves on into what became 'The Scouring of the Shire' without break; Gandalf's departure to seek out Tom Bombadil, where the chapter break would come, was not yet present. When the travellers came to the Brandywine Bridge their reception was just as in RK, but Sam's shouted 'I'll tear your notice down when I find it' is followed by:

'Come along now!' said the wizard. 'My name is Gandalf. And here is a Brandybuck, a Took, a Baggins, and a Gamgee, so if you don't open up quick there will be more trouble than you bargain for, and long before sunrise.'

At that a window slammed, and a crowd of hobbits poured out of the house with lanterns, and they opened the far gate, and some came over the Bridge. When they looked at the travellers they seemed more frightened than ever.

'Come, come,' said Merry, recognizing one of the hobbits. 'If you don't know me, Hob Hayward, you ought to. ...'

Before the narrative had proceeded much further the text was corrected and Gandalf's words were given to Frodo: '"Come along now!" said Frodo. "My name is Frodo Baggins. And here is a Brandybuck, a Took, and a Gamgee..."'

The questioning of Hob Hayward (RK p. 277) is a tangle of names and titles. So far as I can see, it ran thus as first written, with some changes made immediately:

'I'm sorry, Mr. Merry, but we have orders.'
'Whose orders?'
'The Mayor's, Mr. Merry, and the Chief Shirriff's.'
'Who's the Mayor?' said Frodo.
'Mr. [Cosimo >] Sackville of Bag-End.'
'Oh is he, indeed,' said Frodo. 'And who's the Chief Shirriff?'
'Mr. [Baggins >] Sackville of Bag-End.'
'Oh, indeed. Well, I'm glad he's dropped the Baggins at least. And he'll leave Bag-End too if I hear any more nonsense.'

A hush fell on the hobbits beyond the gate. 'It won't do no good to talk that way,' said Hob. 'He'll get to hear of it. And if you make so much noise you'll wake up the Big Man.'

'I'll wake him up in a way that'll surprise him,' said Gandalf. 'If you mean that your precious Mayor is employing ruffians out of the wild, then we've not come back too soon.' He leaped from his horse and put his hand to the gate and tore the notice from it, and threw it on the path in the faces of the hobbits.[1]

This was the last appearance of Gandalf before the final leave-taking at the Grey Havens.[2] 'Gandalf' was changed here to 'Frodo', and 'horse' to 'pony', and it was presumably at this point that the note given on p. 77 ('Gandalf should stay at Bree ...') was written on the manuscript. It will be seen in what follows that in this original version of the story Frodo played a far more aggressive and masterful part in the events than he does in RK, even to the slaying of more than one of the ruffians at Bywater and their leader at Bag End, despite his words to Sam already present in the first manuscript of 'The Land of Shadow' (p. 32; RK p. 204): 'I do not think it is my part to strike any blows again' (see the added sentence given in note 23).

The account of the hobbits' lodging that night in the guard-house by the Brandywine Bridge is much as in the final form, but lacks a few details (as Hob Hayward's remark that stocks of pipe-weed had been 'going away quietly' even before Frodo and his companions left the Shire, and the remonstrance of other hobbits against Hob's indiscretion, RK p. 279). It is Frodo, not Merry, who threatens Bill Ferny and gets rid of him. In the story of their 'arrest' at Frogmorton[3] 'one of the Shirriffs' told them that on the orders of the Chief Shirriff (see note 1) they were to be taken to the *Lock-holes* in Michel Delving (cf. RK p. 280), which is where the term first appears (see pp. 98–9). It turns out that, unlike the later story, Robin Smallburrow was actually the leader of the band of Shirriffs (see p. 95):

To the discomfiture of the Shirriffs Frodo and his companions all roared with laughter. 'Go on,' said Frodo. 'Robin Smallburrow, you're Hobbiton-bred. Don't be silly. But if you're going our way we'll go with you as quiet as you could wish.'

'Which way be you going, Mister Baggins?' said Shirriff Smallburrows,[4] a grin appearing on his face which he quickly smoothed away.

'Hobbiton, of course,' said Frodo. 'Bag End. But you needn't come any further than you wish.'

'Very well, Mr. Baggins,' said the Shirriff, 'but don't forget we've arrested you.'

Sam's conversation with Robin Smallburrows was concluded more abruptly in A (cf. RK pp. 281–2):

'... You know how I went for a Shirriff seven years ago, before all this. Gave you a chance of walking round the Shire and seeing folk and hearing the news, and keeping an eye on the inns. But we all has to swear to do as the Mayor bids. That was all right in the days of old Flourdumpling. Do you remember him? – old Will Whitfoot of Michel Delving. But it's different now. Yet we still has to swear.'

'You shouldn't,' said Sam, 'you should cut out the Shirriffing.'

'Not allowed to,' said Robin.

'If I hear "not allowed" much oftener,' said Sam, 'I'm going to get angry.'

'Can't say I'd be sorry to see it,' said Robin, and he dropped his voice. 'Tell you the truth, your coming back and Mr. Frodo and all is the best that's happened in a year. The Mayor's in a fine taking.'

'He'll be in a fine getting before many days are over,' said Sam.

The Shire-house[5] at Frogmorton was as bad as the gatehouses. ...

It was Frodo, not Merry, who made the Shirriffs march in front on the journey from Frogmorton, and there is no mention of his looking 'rather sad and thoughtful' as his companions laughed and sang. The incident of the old 'gaffer' by the wayside who laughed at the absurd scene, and Merry's refusal to allow the Shirriffs to molest him, is absent;[6] but when the Shirriffs gave up their forced march at the Three-Farthing Stone while Frodo and his friends rode on to Bywater, the leader saying that they were breaking arrest and he could not be answerable, it was again Frodo, not Pippin, who said 'We'll break a good many things yet, and not ask you to answer.'

The horror especially of Frodo and Sam when they came to Bywater and saw what had been done there is told in A very much as in the final form; but from Sam's words 'I want to find the Gaffer' (RK p. 283) I give the text in full, for differences now begin to multiply, and before long the story evolves in a way totally unlike that of the final form of the chapter. By this point my father's handwriting is of extraordinary difficulty, and gets worse; it has been a struggle to elucidate it even to the extent that it is printed here. I have supplied much of the punctuation, and I have silently entered omitted words where these are obvious, corrected words given wrong endings, and so forth.

'It'll be dark, Sam, before we can get there,' said Frodo. 'We'll get there in the morning. One night now won't make any difference.'

'I wish we'd turned down into Buckland first,' said Merry. 'I feel trouble's ahead. We'd have heard all the news there and got some help. Whatever Cosimo's been up to it can't have gone far in Buckland. Bucklanders wouldn't stand any dictating from him!'

All the houses were shut and no one greeted them. And they wondered why, till coming to the Green Dragon, almost the last house on the Hobbiton side, they were astonished and disturbed to see four ill-favoured men lounging at the street-end. Squint-eyed fellows like the one they saw at Bree. 'And at Isengard too,' muttered Merry. They had clubs in their hands and horns in their belts. When they saw the travellers they left the wall they had been leaning on and walked into the road, blocking the way.

'Where do you think you're going?' said one. 'This ain't the road to Michel Delving. And where's the perishing Shirriffs?'

'Coming along nicely,' said Frodo. 'A bit footsore maybe. We'll wait for them.'

'Garn, I told the Boss [> Big Sharkey] it was no good sending the little fools. We ought to have a'gone, but the Boss [> Sharkey] says no, and .... [> the Boss let him have his way.][7]

'And if you had gone, what difference would that have made, pray?' said Frodo quietly. 'We are not used to footpads in this country, but we know how to deal with them.'

'Footpads, eh,' said the man, 'so that's your tone, is it? I'll learn you manners if you ain't careful. Don't you trust too much to the Boss's kind heart. [*Added in margin:* He's all right if you treat him right, but he won't stand talk of that sort.] He's soft enough. But he's only a hobbit. And this country needs something a bit bigger to keep it in order. It'll get it, too, and before the year's out, or my name's not Sharkey. Then you'll learn a thing or two, you little rat-folk.'

'Well,' said Frodo, 'I find that very interesting. I was thinking of waiting here and calling in the morning, but now I think I had better call on the Boss at once, if you mean my cousin Mr. Cosimo. He'd like to know what's afoot in good time.'

The squinting man laughed. 'Oh, he knows alright though he pretends not to. When we've finished with bosses we get rid of them. And of anyone who gets in our way, see?' [*Added in margin, as a replacement or variant:* 'O, Cosimo,' he said, and he laughed again and looked sidelong at his mates. 'Ah, Boss

Cosimo! [*Struck out:* He knows all right, or he did.] Don't you worry about him. He sleeps sound, and I shouldn't try and wake him now. But we're not going to let you pass. We get enough of .... in our way.']

'Yes, I see,' said Frodo. 'I'm beginning to see a great deal. But I fear you're behind the times and the news here, Ruffian Sharkey. Your day's over. You come from Isengard, I think. Well, I have myself come from the South, and this news may concern you. The Dark Tower has fallen, there is a King in Gondor, Isengard is no more, and Saruman is a beggar in the wilderness. You are the fingers of a hand that has been cut off, and arm and body too are dead. The King's messengers will be coming soon up the Greenway, not bullies of Isengard.'

The man stared at him, taken aback for a moment. Then he sneered. 'Swagger it, swagger it, little cock-a-whoop on your pony,' he said. 'Big words and fat lies won't scare us. King's messengers?' he said. 'When I see them I'll take notice maybe.'

This was too much for Pippin. As he thought of the minstrel upon Kormallen and the praise of all the fair host, and here this squint-eyed rascal calling the Ringbearer little cock-a-whoop. [*sic*]

He flashed out his sword and rode forward, casting aside his cloak so that the silver and sable of Gondor which he still wore could be seen. 'We are the King's messengers,' he said. '[And I'm the squire of Frodo of the Nine Fingers, Knight of Gondor, and down you go in the road on your knees or we'll deal with you. >] And I am the esquire of the Lord of Minas Tirith, and here is Frodo of the Nine Fingers renowned among all peoples of the West. You're a fool. Down on your knees in the road, or I'll set this troll's bane in you.' His sword glinted red in the last rays of the sun. Merry and Sam drew and rode up beside him; but Frodo made no move.

The man and his fellows taken aback by the weapons and the sudden fierce speech gave way and ran off up the road to Hobbiton, but they blew their horns as they ran.

'Well, we've come back none too soon,' said Merry.

'Not a day too soon,' said Frodo. 'Poor Cosimo. I hope we haven't sealed his doom.'

'What do you mean, Frodo?' said Pippin. 'Poor Cosimo?   ... I'd seal his doom if I could get at him.'

'I don't think you understand it all quite,' said Frodo. 'Though you should. You've been in Isengard. But I've had

Gandalf to talk to, and we've talked much on the long miles. Poor Cosimo! Well, yes. He's both wicked and silly. But he's caught in his own net. Can't you see? He started trading with Saruman and got rich secretly and bought up this and that on the quiet, and then he's [?hired] these ruffians. Saruman sent them to "help" him, and show him how to build and [??repair] ... all ...   And now of course they're running things in his name – and not in his name for long. He's a prisoner [?really] in Bag End, I expect.'

'Well, I am staggered,' said Pippin. 'Of all the ends to our journey this is the last I expected: to fight half-orcs in the Shire itself to rescue Cosimo the Pimple of all people!'[8]

'Fight?' said Merry. 'Well, it looks like it. But we're after all only 4 hobbits even if we're armed. We don't know how many ruffians there are about. I think we may really need the sledgehammer for this nut after all.'[9]

'Well, we can't help Cousin Pimple tonight,' said Frodo. 'We must find cover for the night.'

'I've an idea, Mr. Frodo,' said Sam. 'Let's go to old Jeremy Cotton's.[10] He used to be a stout fellow, and he has a lot of lads, all friends of mine.'

'What, Farmer Cotton down South Lane?' said Frodo. 'We'll try it!' They turned and a few yards back rode into the lane, and in a quarter of a mile came to the gates. Though it was early all the farmhouse was dark, and not a dog barked. ' "Not allowed", I suppose,' grunted Sam. They knocked on the door, twice. Then slowly a window was opened just above and a head peered out.

'Nay, it's none o' them ruffians,' whispered a voice. 'It's only hobbits.'

'Don't you pay no heed anyway, Jeremy,' said a voice (the farmer's wife by the sound of it). 'It'll only bring trouble, and we've had enough.'

'Go away, there's good fellows,' said the farmer hoarsely. 'Not the front door anyway. If there's anything you want badly come round to the back first thing in the morning before they're about. There's a lot in the street now.'

'We know that,' said Frodo. 'But we've sent them off. It's Mr. Frodo Baggins and friends here. We've come back. But we want shelter for a night. The barn will do.'

'Mr. Frodo Baggins?' gasped the farmer. 'Aye, and Sam with him,' added Sam.

'All right! But don't shout,' said the farmer. 'I'm coming down.'

The bolts were drawn back stealthily and it crossed Sam's mind that he had never known that door to be locked let alone bolted before. Farmer Cotton put a head round and looked at them in the gloaming. His eyes grew round as he looked at them and then grave. 'Well,' he said, 'voices sound all right, but I wouldn't a' knowed you. Come in.' There was dim light in the passage, and he scanned their faces closely. 'Right enough,' he said, and laughed with relief. 'Mr. Baggins and Sam and Mr. Merry and Mr. Pippin. Well, you're welcome, more than welcome. But it's a sorry homecoming. You've been away too long.'

'What's come of my gaffer?' said Sam anxiously.

'Not too well, but not too bad,' said Farmer Cotton. 'He's in one of [?they new] Shire-houses, but he comes to my backdoor and I sees he's better fed than some of the poor things. He's not too bad.'

Sam drew a breath of relief. 'Shire-houses,' he said. 'I'll burn the lot down yet.'

They went into the kitchen and sat down by the fire, which the farmer blew up to a blaze. 'We go to bed early these days,' he said. 'Lights o'night bring unwelcome questions. And these ruffians, they lurk about at night and lie abed late. Early morning's our best time.'

They talked for a while and learned that Frodo's guesses had been near the mark. There were some twenty ruffians quartered in Hobbiton, and Cosimo was up at Bag End; but was never seen outside of it. 'His ma, they took her and put her in the Lockholes at Michel Delving three [?months] ago,' said the farmer. 'I'm less sorry for her than I am for some as they've took. But she did stand up to them proper, there's no denying. Ordered them out of the house, and so they took her.'

'Hm,' said Frodo. 'Then I am afraid we've brought you trouble. For we've threatened four of them and sent them off. The chief of them is one Sharkey by his own naming. I feared there were more. They blew horns and went off.'

'Ah, I heard 'em,' said the farmer. 'That's why we shut down. They'll be after you soon enough, unless you've scared 'em more than I guess. Not but what I think they'd run quick enough from anything of their own size. We'd clear 'em out of the country if only we'd get together.'

'Have they got any weapons?'

'They don't show 'em, no more than whips, clubs, and knives, enough for their dirty work,' said the farmer. 'But maybe they have. Some have got bows and arrows, anyhow, and shoot [?pretty quick] and straight. They've shot three in this district to my knowledge.' Sam ground his teeth.

There came a great bang at the front door. The farmer went quietly down the passage putting out the light and the others followed him. There was a second louder bang. 'Open up you old rat, or we'll burn you out,' shouted a hoarse voice outside.

'I am coming,' said the farmer, all of a [?quake.] 'Slip up and see how many there is,' said Sam. And he [?rattled the chains] and . . . . ed the bolts as the farmer ran up the stairs and back.

'I should say a dozen at the least, but all the lot, I guess,' he said.

'All the better,' said Frodo. 'Now for it.'

The four hobbits stood back to the wall towards which the door swung. The farmer [?unbolted] the bolts, turned the key, and then [?slipped back] up the stairs. The door swung open and in [?peered] the head and shoulders of Sharkey. They let him come in; and then quickly Frodo drove the point of his sword into his neck. He fell, and there was a howl of rage outside. 'Burn them, burn them,' voices cried, 'go and get fuel.' 'Nar, dig them out,' said two, and thrust into the passage. They had swords in their hands, but Frodo now behind the door swung it suddenly in the face of the rear one, while . . . Sam ran Sting through the other.[11] Then the hobbits leaped out. The ruffian who had been down on his face was [?leaning against the doorpost]. He fled, blood pouring from his nose. The farmer . . . took the sword from the fallen ruffian and stood guard at the door. The hobbits ranged about the yards stealthily. They came on two ruffians bringing wood from the woodpile and . . . . ed and killed them before they knew they were attacked. 'It is like a rat hunt,' said Sam. 'But that's only four and one with a broken nose.'

At that moment they heard Merry shouting, 'Gondor to the Mark', and they ran and found him in a corner of the stack yard with four ruffians [?pressing] on him, but held at bay by his sword. They had only knives and clubs. Frodo and Sam came running from one side and Pippin from another. The ruffians fled blowing horns, but one more fell to Frodo's sword before he could escape.

They heard the farmer calling. They ran back. 'One less,' said Farmer Cotton. 'I got him as he ran. The rest have run off down the lane blowing like a hunt.'

'That's six altogether,' said Frodo. 'But no doubt the horns will bring more. How many are there in the neighbourhood?'

'Not many,' said the farmer. 'They mostly bide here or at Michel Delving, and go anywhere's there's any dirty work. No more of [?them's] come in since last spring. I ... say there's not much [more than] a hundred in the whole Shire. If we could only join together.'

'Then let's start tonight,' said Frodo. 'Rouse up the folk. Put lights in the houses. Get out all the lads and grown hobbits. Block the road south and send out scouts round the place.'

It was not long before all Bywater was alive and awake again. Lights shining in windows and people at their doors. And there were even cheers for Mr. Frodo. Some lit a bonfire at the Road Bend[12] and danced round it. It was after all not more than [the] six[th of] October[13] on a fair evening of late autumn. Others went off to spy the land round about.

Those that went up Hobbiton way said that there was quite a hubbub there. News of Mr. Frodo's return had come in and folk were coming out. The ruffians seemed to have left the place clear. 'Bolted towards Michel Delving where they've made the Lockholes into a fortress, that's what they've a' done, I guess,' said Farmer Cotton. 'But they'll come back. There's no way from the West.[14] They don't go down the Tuckborough way. They've never given in there. And they've [?beaten] up more than one ruffian in the Took-house.[15] There is a kind o' siege going on.'

'We'll send word to them. Who'll go?' No answer.

'I'll go of course,' said Pippin. 'It's my own country. I'm proud of it. It's not more than 14 miles, as the crow flies or as Took goes who knows all the ways, from here where I stand to the Long Smial of [?Tuckborough] where I was born.[16] Anyone come with me? Well, never mind. I'll be bringing some [?stout] Tooklanders this way in the morning.'

Frodo sent out other messengers to all hamlets and farms near enough for folk to be willing to run to them.

Nothing more that night.

In the morning from Hobbiton and Bywater and round about there were about 100 fullgrown hobbits gathered together with sticks, staves, knives, pitchforks and mattocks and axes and scythes. Messages came in to say that a dozen or more ruffians had been seen going west to Michel Delving the evening before. Then a hobbit ran in to say that about fifty Tooklanders had come in on ponies to the East Road junction and a couple of hundred were marching up behind. 'Whole country's up, like a fire,' he said. 'It's grand! Right glad we are you came back, Mr. Frodo. That's what we needed.'

Frodo now had forces enough. He had [?the] block .. ... the East .....[17] and put a lot of them behind the hedge on each side of the way. They were under Pippin's command. 'I don't know what you think,' he said to Merry and Sam. 'But it seems to me that either the ruffians are all going to gather in Michel Delving and fight it out there: in that case we'll have to raise the Shire and go and dig them out; or more likely they'll come back in full force this way to their precious Boss. It's forty miles if it's a foot to Michel Delving. Unless they get ponies (which wouldn't help much) or have got horses they can't come back for a day or two.'

'They'll send a messenger,' said Sam, 'and wait somewhere till their friends arrive; that'll speed things up a bit. Even so I don't see how they can do it till the day after tomorrow at quickest.'

'Well then,' said Frodo, 'we'd best spend the time by going to Hobbiton and have a word with Cousin Cosimo.'

'Right you are, Mr. Frodo,' said Sam, 'and I'll look up the gaffer.'

So leaving Pippin in charge on the Road and Farmer Cotton in Bywater, Frodo, Sam and Merry rode on to Hobbiton. It was one of the saddest days of their lives. The great chimney rose up before them, and as they came in sight of the village they saw that the old mill was gone and a great red brick building straddled the stream. All along the Bywater road every tree was felled, and little ugly houses with no gardens in [?desert] ..... of ash or gravel. As they looked up the hill they gasped. The old farm on the right had been turned into a [?long ?big] work-shop or [?building] with many new windows. The chestnuts were gone. Bagshot Row was a yawning sand-pit, and Bag End up beyond could not be seen for a row of sheds and ugly huts.[18]

[*The following was struck out and replaced immediately:* A [?surly dirty] ill-favoured hobbit was lounging at the new mill-door. He was [?smut]-faced and [?chewing]. 'As good a small model of Bill Ferny as I've seen,' said Sam.

Ted Sandyman did not seem to recognize them but stared at them with a leer until they had nearly passed.

'Going to see the Boss?' he said. 'It's a bit early. But you'll see the notice on the gate. Are you the folks that have been making all the row down at Bywater? If you are, I shouldn't [?try] the Boss. He's angry. Take my advice and sheer off. You're not wanted. We've got work to do in the Shire now and we don't want noisy riffraff.'

'You don't always get what you want, Ted Sandyman,' said Sam. 'And I can tell you what's coming to you, whether you like it or no: a bath.' He jumped from his pony and before the astonished Ted knew what was coming Sam hit him square on the nose, and lifting him with an effort threw him over the bridge with a splash.]

A dirty surly-looking hobbit was lounging on the bridge by the mill. He was grimy-faced and grimy-handed, and was chewing. 'As good a small copy of Bill Ferny as you could ask for!' said Sam. 'So that's what Ted Sandyman admires, is it. I'm not surprised.'

Ted looked at him and spat. 'Going to see the Boss?' he said. 'If you are you're too early. He don't see no visitors till eleven, not even them as thinks themselves high and mighty. And he won't see you anyway. You're for the Lockholes, where you belong. Take my advice and sheer off before they come for you. We don't want you. We've work to do in the Shire now.'

'So I see,' said Sam. 'No time for a bath, but time for wall-propping. Well, never you mind, Ted, we'll find you something to do before this year's much older. And in the meantime keep your mouth shut. I've a score to pay in this village, and don't you make it any longer with your sneers, or you'll foot a bill too big for you to pay.'

Ted laughed. 'You're out o' date, Mr. Samwise, with your elves and your dragons. If I were you I'd go and catch one of them ships that [are] [?always] sailing, according to your tale. Go back to Babyland and rock your cradle, and don't bother us. We're going to make a big town here with twenty mills. A hundred new houses next year. Big stuff coming up from the South. Chaps who can work metals, and make big holes in the ground. There'll be forges a-humming and [?steamwhistles] and wheels going round. Elves can't do things like that.'

Sam looked at him, and his retorts died on his lips. He shook his head.

'Don't worry, Sam,' said Frodo. 'He's day-dreaming, poor wretch. And he's right behind the times. Let him be. But what we shall do with [him] is a bit of a worry. I hope there's not many caught the disease.'

'If I had known all the mischief Saruman had been up to,' said Merry, 'I'd have stuffed my pouch down his throat.'

They went sadly up the winding road to Bag End. The Field of the Party was all hillocks, as if moles had gone mad in it, but by some miracle the tree was still standing, now forlorn and nearly leafless.[19] They came at last to the door. The bell-chain dangled loose. No bell could be rung, no knocking was answered. At last they pushed and the door opened. They went in. The place stank, it was full of filth and disorder, but it did not appear to have been lived in for some time. 'Where is that miserable Cosimo hiding?' they said. There was nothing living to be found in any room save mice and rats.

'This is worse than Mordor,' said Frodo. 'Much worse in some ways.' 'Ah,' said Sam, 'it goes home as they say, because this is home, and it's all so, so mean, dirty [and] shabby. I'm very sorry, Mr. Frodo. But I'm glad I didn't know before. All the time in the bad places we've been in I've had the Shire in mind, and that's what I've rested on, if you take my meaning. I'd not have had a hope if I'd known all this.'

'I understand,' said Frodo. 'I said much the same to Gandalf long ago.[20] Never mind, Sam. It's our task to put it all right again. Hard work, but we'll not mind. Your box will come in useful.'

'My box?' said Sam. 'Glory and sunshine, Mr. Frodo, but of course. She knew, of course she knew. Showed me a bit in the Mirror. Bless her. I'd well-nigh forgotten it. But let's find that Boss first.'

'Hi you, what're you doing? Come out of it!' A loud voice rang out. They ran to the door and saw a large man, bowlegged, squinteyed, [?painfully ??bent] coming up the field from one of the sheds. 'What in Mordor do you mean by it?' he shouted. 'Come out of it. Come here, you Shire-rats. I [?saw] you.'

They came out and went to meet him. When they drew near enough for him to see them he stopped and looked at them, and to Frodo it seemed that he was .... [?and] a little afraid. 'We're looking for the Boss,' he said, 'or so I think you call him. Mr. Cosimo of Bag End. I'm his cousin. I used to live here.'

'Hi lads, hi, [?come here],' shouted the man. 'Here they are. We've got 'em.'

But there was no answer.

Frodo smiled. 'I think, Ruffian Sharkey, [?we] should cry "We've got him"? If you're calling for your other ruffians I'm afraid they've made off. To Michel Delving, I'm told. I am told you sleep sound.[21] Well, what about it now.' The hobbits drew their swords and pressed near him; but he backed away. Very orc-like all his movements were, and he stooped now with his hands nearly touching the ground. 'Blast and grind the fools,' he said. 'Why didn't they warn me?'

'They thought of themselves first, I expect,' said Frodo, 'and anyway you've given strict orders that your sleep is not to be disturbed. It's on every notice. Come. I want to see the Boss. Where is he?'

The man looked puzzled. Then he laughed. 'You're looking at him,' he said. 'I'm the Boss. I'm Sharkey all right.'

'Then where is Mr. Cosimo of Bag End?'

'Don't ask me,' said the man. 'He saw what was coming, and he legged it one night. Poor booby. But it saved us the trouble of wringing his neck. We'd had enough of him. And we've got on better without him. He hadn't the guts of his ma.'

'I see,' said Frodo. 'So you ruffians from Isengard have been bullying this country for a year, and [??pretending] to be Mayor and Shirriff and what not, and eating most of the food and ...ing folk and setting up your filthy hutches. What for?'

'Who are you,' said the man, 'to "what for" me? I'm the Boss. And I do what I like. These little swine have got to learn how to work and I'm here to learn 'em. Saruman wants goods and he wants provisions, and he wants a lot of things lying idle here. And he'll get them, or we'll screw the necks of all you little rats and take the land for ourselves.'

'Isengard is a ruin and Saruman walks as a beggar,' said Frodo. 'You've outlived your time, Ruffian Sharkey. The Dark Tower has fallen and there is a King in Gondor, and there is a King also in the North. We come from the King. I give you three days. After that you are outlaw, and if you're found in this Shire you shall be killed, as you killed the [?wretch] Cosimo. I see in your eye that you lie, and in your hands that you strangled him. Your way leads downhill and [to] the East. Quick now!'

The orc-man looked at them with such a leer of hatred as they had not seen even in all their adventures. '... you're liars like all your kind. Elf-friends and . . . . And four to one, which makes you so bold.'

'Very well,' said Frodo, 'one to one.' He took off his cloak. Suddenly he shone, a small gallant figure clad in mithril like an elf-prince. Sting was in his hand;[22] but he was not much more than half Sharkey's stature. Sharkey had a sword, and he drew it, and in a [?fury] hewed double-handed at Frodo. But Frodo using the advantage of his size and [?courage] ran in close holding his cloak as a shield and slashed his leg above the knee. And then as with a groan and a curse the orc-man [?toppled] over him he stabbed upwards, and Sting passed clean through his body.

So died Sharkey the Boss [?on the] . . . . where Bilbo's garden had been. Frodo [??crawling] from under him looked at him as he wiped Sting on the grass. 'Well,' he said, 'if ever Bilbo hears of this he'll believe the world has really changed! When Gandalf and I sat here long ago, I think that at least one thing I could never have guessed would be that the last stroke of the battle would be at this door.'[23]

'Why not?' said Sam. 'Very right and proper. And I'm glad that it was yours, Mr. Frodo. But if I may say so, though it was a grand day at Kormallen, and the happiest I have known, I never have felt that you got as much praise as you deserve.'

'Of course not, Sam,' said Frodo. 'I'm a hobbit. But why grumble? You've been far more neglected yourself. There's never only one hero in any true tale, Sam, and all the good folk are in others' debt. But if one had to choose one and one only, I'd choose Samwise.'

'Then you'd be wrong, Mr. Frodo,' said Sam. 'For without you I'm nothing. But you and me together, Mr. Frodo: well, that's more than either alone.'

'It's more than anything I've heard of,' said Merry. 'But as for the last stroke of battle, I'm not so sure. You've finished the beastly Boss, while I only looked on. I've a [?feeling] from the horns in the distance you'll find that Pippin and the Tooks have had the last word. Thank heaven my . . . . . is Took Brandybuck.'

It was as he said. While they had dealt with the Boss things had flared up in Bywater. The ruffians were no fools. They had sent a man on a horse to [?within] horn cry of Michel Delving (for they had many horn-signals). By midnight they had all assembled at Waymoot,[24] 18 miles west of the Bywater Road [?crossing]. They had [?horses of their own] on the White

Downs and rode like the fire. They charged the road-barrier at
10 a.m. but fifty were slain. The others had scattered and
escaped. Pippin had killed [?five] and was wounded himself.

So ended the [??fierce] battle of Bywater, the only battle ever
fought in the Shire. And it has at least a chapter all to itself in all
standard histories.

It was some time before the last ruffians were hunted out.
And oddly enough, little though the hobbits were inclined to
believe it, quite a number turned out to be far from incurable.

This ends a page, and with it the now fearsomely difficult writing
comes to an end: for the next page is perfectly legible, and this better
script continues to the end of the draft, which is also the end of *The
Lord of the Rings*. The pagination is continuous, however, and the
likeliest explanation seems to be that there was simply a break in
composition at this point.
The division between 'The Scouring of the Shire' and 'The Grey
Havens' occurs at a point in RK that has nothing corresponding in the
original draft, but it is convenient to make a break here, after one
further paragraph concerning the fate of the 'ruffians', and to give the
further continuation of the draft in the following chapters.

If they gave themselves up they were kindly treated, and fed
(for they were usually half-starved after hiding in the woods),
and then shown to the borders. This sort were Dunlanders, not
orc-men/halfbreeds, who had originally come because their
own land was wretched, and Saruman had told them there was
a good country with plenty to eat away North. It is said that
they found their own country very much better in the days of
the King and were glad to return; but certainly the reports that
they spread (enlarged for the covering of their own shame) of
the numerous and warlike, not to say ferocious, hobbits of the
Shire did something to preserve the hobbits from further
trouble.

It is very striking that here, virtually at the end of *The Lord of the
Rings* and in an element in the whole that my father had long
meditated, the story when he first wrote it down should have been so
different from its final form (or that he so signally failed to see 'what
really happened'!). And this is not only because the original story took
a wrong direction, as it turned out, when all four of the 'travellers'
went to Farmer Cotton's house, nor because he did not perceive that it
was Saruman who was the real 'Boss', Sharkey, at Bag End, but most
of all because Frodo is portrayed here at every stage as an energetic
and commanding intelligence, warlike and resolute in action; and the

final text of the chapter had been very largely achieved when the changed conception of Frodo's part in the Scouring of the Shire entered.

It is perhaps a minor question, to try to resolve how my father was developing the idea of 'Sharkey' as he wrote this text, but it is certainly not easy to do so. The statements made are as follows:

– The chief of the orcish men at Bywater said (p. 82) that he had told the Boss that it was no good sending hobbits, and that the men ought to have gone, but the Boss had said no. This was changed to make the man say that he had given this advice to 'Big Sharkey', but Sharkey had said no, and 'the Boss let him have his way'.

– Later in the same conversation, this man says: 'It'll get it too, and before the year's out, or my name's not Sharkey.' Then Frodo calls him (p. 83) 'Ruffian Sharkey'.

– When the ruffians came to Farmer Cotton's house it was 'Sharkey' who peered in at the door; and Frodo slew him with his sword.

– The man who accosted the hobbits at Bag End (whose orc-like character is much emphasised) is called by Frodo 'Ruffian Sharkey' (p. 91).

– Frodo tells this man that he wants to see the Boss; to which he replies: 'I'm the Boss. I'm Sharkey all right.'

– Subsequently Frodo again calls him 'Ruffian Sharkey'; and he slays him with Sting in single combat.

As the text stands there can be no solution to this unless it is supposed that my father changed his conception as he wrote without altering the earlier passages. This would probably mean that the name 'Sharkey', whatever its basis as a name, was transferred from the squint-eyed rascal at Bywater when my father saw that 'the Boss' (Cosimo Sackville-Baggins) was being used now purely nominally by some more ruthless and sinister presence at Bag End: this was 'Sharkey'.[25] Then, suddenly, after the present draft was completed, my father saw who it really was that had supplanted Cosimo, and Saruman took over the name 'Sharkey'.[26]

At any rate, it is altogether certain that Saruman only entered the Shire in person in the course of the development of the present chapter. On the other hand, his previous baleful association with Cosimo Sackville-Baggins was present in the original draft, as is seen from Frodo's remarks at Bywater (p. 84) and Merry's at Bag End (p. 90: 'If I had known all the mischief Saruman had been up to, I'd have stuffed my pouch down his throat').

It required much further work to attain the story as it stands in *The Return of the King*, and the vehicle of this development was the complicated second manuscript 'B', which was numbered 'LIX' and at first given the title 'The Mending of the Shire'. It seems very probable that Saruman's presence at Bag End had already arisen when my

father began writing this text, and the references to 'Sharkey' are as in
RK; but while in detail and in wording it advances far towards the
final form he was still following A in certain features, and the major
shift in the plot (whereby the fight at Farmer Cotton's house was
removed) took place in the course of the writing of the manuscript.

Before that point in the story is reached the most notable feature is
that Frodo retains his dominance and his resolute captaincy. The
incident of the old 'gaffer' who jeered at the band of Shirriffs on their
forced march from Frogmorton entered in B, but it was Frodo, not
Merry, who sharply ordered their leader to leave him alone. The
leader was still, and explicitly, Robin Smallburrow (' "Smallburrow!"
said Frodo. "Order your fellows back to their places at once" '); but
his displacement by the officious and anonymous leader took place in
the course of the writing of this manuscript.[27]

There was a notable development in B of Frodo's exposition to
Pippin concerning Cosimo and Saruman and the pass to which the
Shire has been brought (see pp. 83–4). This was removed (cf. RK
p. 285) when, on a rider inserted into B, it became Farmer Cotton who
recounted from personal knowledge the recent history; but Cotton, of
course, did not know who Sharkey was, and presumably would not
have been much enlightened to learn that he was Saruman.

'I don't think you understand it quite,' said Frodo. 'Though
you were at Isengard, and have heard all that I have since. Yes,
Poor Cosimo! He has been a wicked fool. But he's caught in his
own net now. Don't you see? Saruman became interested in us
and in the Shire a good while ago, and began spying. [*Added:* So
Gandalf said.] A good many of the strange folk that had been
prowling about for a long while before we started must have
been sent by him. I suppose he got into touch with Cosimo that
way. Cosimo was rich enough, but he always did want more. I
expect he started trading with Saruman, and getting richer
secretly, and buying up this and that on the quiet. [*Added:*
Saruman needed supplies for his war.]'

'Ah!' said Sam, 'tobacco, a weakness of Saruman's. [> 'Yes!'
said Pippin. 'And tobacco for himself and his favourites!] I
suppose that Cosimo must have got his hands on most of it. And
on the South-farthing fields, too, I shouldn't wonder.'

'I expect so,' said Frodo. 'But he soon got bigger ideas than
that. He began hiring [> He seems to have hired] ruffians; or
Saruman sent them to him, to "help him". Chimneys, tree-
hacking, all those shoddy little houses. They look like imitations
of Saruman's notions of "improvement". But now, of course,
the ruffians are on top ...'

The text then becomes that of RK; but after Frodo's admonition on the subject of killing (RK p. 285) it continues thus, following and expanding A (p. 84):

'It depends on how many of these ruffians there are,' said Merry. 'If there are a lot, then it will certainly mean fighting, Frodo. And it isn't going to be as easy after this. It may prove a nut tough enough for Gandalf's sledgehammer. After all we're only four hobbits, even if we're armed.'

'Well, we can't help Cousin Pimple tonight,' said Pippin; 'we need to find more out. You heard that horn-blowing? There's evidently more ruffians near at hand. We ought to get under cover soon. Tonight will be dangerous.'

'I've an idea,' said Sam. 'Let's go to old Cotton's. He always was a stout fellow, and he's a lot of lads that were all friends of mine.'

'D'you mean Farmer Cotton down South Lane?' said Frodo. 'We'll try him!'

They turned, and a few yards back came on South Lane leading out of the main road; in about a quarter of a mile it brought them to the farmer's gates.

In the story of their arrival at the farm, their welcome there and conversation with Farmer Cotton, my father followed A (pp. 84–6) closely, with some minor expansion but no movement away from the draft narrative (except that the imprisonment of Lobelia Sackville-Baggins is made longer: '"They took his ma six months ago," said Cotton, "end o' last April"'). But from the bang on the front door the story changes:

There came at that moment a loud bang on the door. Farmer Cotton went softly down the passage, putting out the light. The others followed. There was a second louder bang.

'Open up, you old rat, or we'll burn you out!' shouted a hoarse voice outside. Mrs. Cotton in a nearby room stifled a scream. Down the stairs that led into the kitchen five young hobbits came clattering from the two upper rooms where they slept. They had thick sticks, but nothing more.

'I'm coming,' shouted the farmer, rattling the chains and making a to-do with the bolts. 'How many is there?' he whispered to his sons. 'A dozen at least,' said Young Tom, the eldest, 'maybe all the lot.'

'All the better,' said Frodo. 'Now for it! Open up and then get back. Don't join in, unless we need help badly.'

The four hobbits with swords drawn stood back to the wall against which the door swung. There came a great blow on the lock, but at that moment the farmer drew the last bolt, and slipped back with his sons some paces down the passage [added: and round the corner out of sight]. The door opened slowly and in peered the head of the ruffian they had already met. He stepped forward, stooping, holding a sword in his hand. As soon as he was well inside, the hobbits, who were now behind the opened door, flung it back with a crash. While Frodo slipped a bolt back, the three others leaped on the ruffian from behind, threw him down on his face and sat on him. He felt a cold blade of steel at his neck.

'Keep still and quiet!' said Sam. 'Cotton!' called Merry. 'Rope! We've got one. Tie him up!'

But the ruffians outside began attacking the door again, while some were smashing the windows with stones. 'Prisoner!' said Frodo. 'You seem a leader. Stop your men, or you will pay for the damage!'

They dragged him close to the door. 'Go home, you fools!' he shouted. 'They've got me, and they'll do for me, if you go on. Clear out! Tell Sharkey!'

'What for?' a voice answered from outside. 'We know what Sharkey wants. Come on, lads! Burn the whole lot inside! Sharkey won't miss that boob; he's no use for them as makes mistakes. Burn the lot! Look alive and get the fuel!'

'Try again!' said Sam grimly.

The prisoner now desperately frightened screamed out: 'Hi, lads! No burnings! No more burnings, Sharkey said. Send a messenger. You might find it was you as had made a mistake. Hi! D'you hear?'

'All right, lads!' said the other voice. 'Two of you ride back quick. Two go for fuel. The rest make a ring round the place!'

'Well, what's the next move?' said Farmer Cotton. 'At least they won't start burning until they've ridden to Bag-end and back: say half an hour, allowing for some talk. The murdering villains! Never thought they'd start burning. They burned a lot of folk out earlier, but they've not done [any] for a long while. We understood the Boss had stopped it. But see here! I've got the wife and my daughter Rosie to think of.'

'There's only two things to be done,' said Frodo. 'One of us has got to slip out and get help: rouse the folk. There must be

200 grown hobbits not far away. Or else we've got to burst out
in a pack with your wife and daughter in a huddle, and do it
quick, while two are away and before more come.'

'Too much risk for the one [that] slips out,' said Cotton.
'Burst out together, that's the ticket, and make a dash up the
lane.'

The concluding passage, from 'There's only two things to be done,'
was written in a rapidly degenerating scribble, and the text ends here,
not at the foot of a page. The story of the attack on the farmhouse had
already shifted strongly away from that in the original draft (in which
Frodo and Sam slew two of the marauders at the front door and four
others were killed in the yard before the remainder fled); and at this
point my father decided that he had taken a wrong turning. Perhaps he
could not see any credible way in which they could burst out of the
house (with the young Cottons and their mother in the midst) and
through the ring of men unscathed. At any rate, the whole of this part
of the B text, from ' "D'you mean Farmer Cotton down South Lane?"
said Frodo' (p. 96), was removed from the manuscript and replaced by
a new start, with Frodo's saying in response to Sam's suggestion that
they all go to Farmer Cotton's: 'No! It's no good getting "under
cover" ', as in RK (p. 286), where however it is Merry who says this. It
is Frodo also, not Merry, who answers Pippin's question 'Do what?'
with 'Raise the Shire! Now! Wake all our people!', and tells Sam that
he can make a dash for Cotton's farm if he wants to; he ends 'Now,
Merry, you have a horn of the Mark. Let us hear it!'

The story of the return of the four hobbits to the middle of Bywater,
Merry's horn-call, Sam's meeting with Farmer Cotton and his sons, his
visit to Mrs. Cotton and Rose, and the fire made by the villagers, is
told in virtually the same words as in RK (pp. 286–8), the only
difference being that it was on the orders of Frodo, not of Merry, that
barriers were set up across the road at each end of Bywater. When
Farmer Cotton tells that the Boss (as he is still named throughout B,
though emended later to 'the Chief') has not been seen for a week or
two B diverges a little from RK, for Tom Cotton the younger
interrupts his father at this point:

'They took his ma, that Lobelia,' put in Young Tom. 'That'd
be six months back, when they started putting up sheds at Bag
End without her leave. She ordered 'em off. So they took her.
Put her in the Lock-holes. They've took others that we miss
more; but there's no denying she stood up to 'em bolder than
most.'

'That's where most of them are,' said the farmer, 'over at
Michel Delving. They've made the old Lock-holes into a regular

fort, we hear, and they go from there roaming round, "gather-ing". Still I guess that there's no more than a couple of hundred in the Shire all told. We can master 'em, if we stick together.'

'Have they got any weapons?' asked Merry.

This perhaps implies that the *Lock-holes* were a prison in the days before any 'ruffian' came to the Shire. Subsequently Young Tom's story of Lobelia was removed from this part of the narrative, and replaced by Pippin's question 'Hobbiton's not their only place, is it?', which leads into Farmer Cotton's account of where else the 'ruffians' hung out beside Hobbiton, as in RK (p. 288), and a different idea of the origin of the Lock-holes: 'some old tunnels at Michel Delving'.

Merry's question 'Have they got any weapons?' leads, as in RK, to Farmer Cotton's account of the resistance of the Tooks, but without his reference to Pippin's father (Paladin Took), the Thain, and his refusal to have anything to do with the pretensions of Lotho (Cosimo):

'There you are, Frodo!' said Merry. 'I knew we'd have to fight. Well, they started it.'

'Not exactly,' said Farmer Cotton, 'leastways not the shoot-ing. Tooks started that. You see, the Tooks have got those deep holes in the Green Hills, the Smiles[28] as they call 'em, and the ruffians can't come at 'em ...'

With Frodo still firmly in the saddle at Bywater, Merry rode off with Pippin to Tuckborough (as he does not in RK). After they had gone, Frodo reiterated his injunction against any killing that could be avoided (as in RK, p. 289), but then continued: 'We shall be having a visit from the Hobbiton gang very soon. It's over an hour since we sent the four ruffians off from here. Do nothing, until I give the word. Let them come on!' In RK it is Merry who gives the warning that the men from Hobbiton will soon be coming to Bywater, and he concludes 'Now I've got a plan'; to which Frodo merely replies 'Very good. You make the arrangements.' The arrival of the men, and the trapping of them beside the fire where Farmer Cotton was standing apparently all alone, follows exactly as in the final story, except that it is of course Frodo, not Merry, who accosts the leader; and when this encounter is over, and the men bundled off into one of their own huts, Farmer Cotton says 'You came back in the nick, Mr. Frodo.'

Then follows Cotton's account to Sam of the condition of the Gaffer ('he's in one of them new Shire-houses, Boss-houses I call 'em'), and Sam's departure to fetch him, virtually as in RK (p. 291). Once again, it is Frodo not Merry who posts look-outs and guards, and he goes off alone with Farmer Cotton to his house: 'He sat with the family in the kitchen, and they asked a few polite questions, but were far more concerned with events in the Shire. In the middle of the talk in burst

Sam, with the Gaffer.' The farmer's account of the 'troubles', ending with Young Tom's story of the carting off of Lobelia to the Lock-holes (RK p. 291–3), was inserted into B on a long rider; and at this time Frodo's earlier suppositions about how it all began (p. 95) and Young Tom's earlier remarks about Lobelia (p. 98) were removed.[29]

The incursion of the Gaffer into the Cottons' kitchen is told as in RK (pp. 293–4); but then follows in B:

In the morning early they heard the ringing call of Merry's horn, and in marched nearly a hundred of Tooks and other hobbits from Tuckborough and the Green Hills. The Shire was all alight, they said, and the ruffians that prowled round Tookland had fled; east to the Brandywine mostly, pursued by other Tooks.

There were now enough forces for a strong guard on the East Road from Michel Delving to Brandywine, and for another guard in Bywater. When all that had been settled and put in the charge of Pippin, Frodo and Sam and Merry with Farmer Cotton and an escort of fifty set out for Hobbiton.

The text then continues with the story of their coming to Hobbiton and meeting with Ted Sandyman, and their entry into Bag End, told almost word for word as in RK (pp. 296–7);[30] and ends with the advent of Saruman and his murder by Wormtongue (on which see pp. 102–3). The text B ends just as does the chapter in RK, with Merry's saying 'And the very last end of the War, I hope', Frodo's calling it 'the very last stroke', and Sam's saying 'I shan't call it the end, till we've cleared up the mess.' But there is thus no Battle of Bywater!

The Battle is found on inserted pages that are numbered as additional ('19a, 19b') to the consecutive pagination of the text just described. If this pagination means that these pages were written and inserted subsequently, and it is hard to see what else it could mean, it might seem that my father (still following the story in A, in which the visit to Hobbiton preceded the battle, p. 92) had driven on to the end of the Bag End episode without realising that the story of the Battle of Bywater had yet to be told. But this seems incredible. Far more likely he saw, as he wrote the story of the visit to Hobbiton, that the order of the narration in A must be reversed, so that the chapter would end with the last stroke of the War 'at the very door of Bag End'; but he postponed the battle, and inserted it subsequently into the text already continuously paginated.

Whenever this was done, the existing text (in which the dispositions for defence next morning were followed at once by the visit to Hobbiton) was altered to that of RK (p. 294), and the approach of the men along the road from Waymoot and their ambush on the high-banked road to Bywater was told almost as in the final story: the

few differences in this passage are chiefly caused by Merry's having
gone to Tuckborough with Pippin. The messenger from the Tookland
does not refer to the Thain (see p. 99), and tells that 'Mr. Peregrin and
Mr. Merry are coming on with all the folk we can spare'; it was Nick
Cotton, not Merry, who had been out all night and reported the
approach of the men, whom he estimated to number 'fifty or more'
('close on a hundred', RK); and when the Tooks came in 'the ringing
call of Merry's horn was heard.' But from the point where the way
back out of the ambush was blocked against the ruffian men, when the
hobbits pushed out more carts onto the road, the B text diverges
remarkably from the story told in RK:

A voice spoke to them from above. 'Well,' said Frodo, 'you
have walked into a trap. Your fellows from Hobbiton did the
same, and are all prisoners now. Lay down your weapons! Then
go back twenty paces and sit down. Any who try to break out
will be shot.'
Many of the men, in spite of the curses of their more
villainous mates, at once obeyed. But more than a score turned
about and charged back down the lane. Hobbit archers at gaps
in the hedges shot down six before they reached the waggons.
Some of them gave up, but ten or more burst through and
dashed off, and scattered across country making for the Woody
End it seemed.
Merry blew a loud horn-call. There were answering calls
from a distance. 'They won't get far!' he said. 'All that country
is now alive with hunters.'
The dead ruffians were laden on waggons and taken off and
buried in an old gravel-pit nearby, the Battle Pits as they were
called ever afterwards. The others were marched off to the
village to join their fellows.
So ended the Battle of Bywater, 1419, the [only >] last battle
fought in the Shire, and the only battle since the Greenfields,
1137,[31] away up in the North Farthing. In consequence,
although it only cost six ruffian lives and no hobbits it has a
chapter to itself in all the standard histories, and the names of
all those who took part were made into a Roll and learned by
heart. The very considerable rise in the fame and fortunes of the
Cottons dates from this time.

The connection with the visit to Hobbiton was made in these words:

When all was settled, and a late midday meal had been eaten,
Merry said: 'Well now, Frodo, it's time to deal with the Chief.'

Farmer Cotton collected an escort of some fifty sturdy hobbits, and then they set out on foot for Bag End: Frodo, Sam, Merry and Pippin led the way.

The words 'When all was settled' are used now to refer to the ending of the battle and the disposal of the dead and captured ruffians; previously (p. 100) they had referred to the arrangements made to meet the approaching enemy.

The story of the meeting with Saruman at Bag End was written out twice in B, the first form soon declining into a scribble when my father thought better of the opening of the episode. The first opening I give here:

'No doubt, no doubt. But you did not, and so I am able to welcome you home!' There standing at the door was Saruman, looking well-fed and a great deal less wretched than before; his eyes gleamed with malice and amusement.

A sudden light broke on Frodo. 'Sharkey!' he said. Saruman laughed. 'So you've heard that, have you? I believe all my men used to call me that in the better times. They were so devoted. And so it has followed me up here, has it? Really I find that quite cheering.'

'I cannot imagine why,' said Frodo. 'And what are you doing here anyway? Just a little shabby mischief? Gandalf said he thought you were still capable of that.'

[Struck out: 'Need you ask?' said Saruman.] 'You make me laugh, you hobbit lordlings,' said Saruman. 'Riding along with all these great people so secure and so pleased with yourselves; thinking you have done great things and can now just come back and laze in the country. Saruman's home can be ruined, and he can be turned out. But not Mr. Baggins. Oh, no! He's really important.

'But Mr. Baggins is a fool all the same. And can't even mind his own affairs, always minding other people's. To be expected of a pupil of Gandalf. He must dawdle on the way, and ride twice as far as he need. The Shire would be all right. Well, after our little meeting I thought I might get ahead of you and learn you a lesson. It would have been a sharper lesson if only you had dawdled longer. Still I have done a little that you'll find it hard to mend in your time. It'll be a warning to you to leave other folk alone, and not to be so cocksure. And it will give me something quite pleasant to think about, to set against my own injuries.'

The second version of the episode in B is virtually as in RK, except that it entirely lacks any reference to the dreadful corpse of Saruman and the mist that rose above it and loomed 'as a pale shrouded figure' over the Hill of Hobbiton; and this passage did not enter until my father wrote it in on the page proofs of *The Return of the King*.

A note that he pencilled against the episode in a copy of the First Edition is interesting:

Saruman turned back into Dunland[32] on Aug. 28. He then made for the old South Road and then went north over the Greyflood at Tharbad, and thence NW. to Sarn Ford, and so into the Shire and to Hobbiton on Sept. 22: a journey of about 460 [miles] in 25 days. He thus averaged about 18 miles a day – evidently hastening as well as he could. He had thus only 38 days in which to work his mischief in the Shire; but much of it had already been done by the ruffians according to his orders – already planned and issued before the sack of Isengard.

September 22 is the date given in *The Tale of Years* for Saruman's coming to the Shire, and October 30 for the coming of the 'travellers' to the Brandywine Bridge.

At a late stage of work on the B text (but before the insertion of the long rider in which Farmer Cotton recounts the history of the Shire since Frodo and his companions left, see p. 100 and note 29) my father perceived that Frodo's experience had so changed him, so withdrawn him, as to render him incapable of any such rôle in the Scouring of the Shire as had been portrayed. The text as it stood required no large recasting; the entirely different picture of Frodo's part in the events was brought about by many small alterations (often by doing no more than changing 'Frodo' to 'Merry') and a few brief additions. Virtually all of these have been noticed in the foregoing account.

A third, very fine manuscript ('C') followed B, and here the text of RK was reached in all but a few passages, most of these being very minor matters. It was on this manuscript that Cosimo Sackville-Baggins became Lotho, and the references to the Thain were introduced (see pp. 99, 101). The number of men at the Battle of Bywater had been enlarged to 'more than seventy', and the battle had become much fiercer, with the trapped men climbing the banks above the road and attacking the hobbits, already as C was first written; by later emendation the numbers of the men and of the slain on both sides were further increased. The original reading of C 'Merry himself slew the largest of the ruffians' was altered to '... the leader, a great squint-eyed brute like a huge orc'; with this cf. the description of the orc-man 'Sharkey' at Bag End in the A version, pp. 90–1. Lastly, an important addition was made to C concerning Frodo: 'Frodo had been in the battle, but he had not drawn sword, and his chief part had been to prevent the hobbits in their wrath at their losses from slaying those of their enemies who threw down their weapons' (RK pp. 295–6).

There lacked now only the passage describing the departure of the spirit of Saruman, and his corpse.

NOTES

1 Subsequently the passage was corrected in pencil. The question 'Who's the Mayor?' was given to Merry, and the answer became 'The Boss at Bag End'; Frodo's 'And who's the Chief Shirriff?' received the same answer. Then follows: 'Boss? Boss? You mean Mr. Cosimo, I suppose.' 'I suppose so, Mr. Baggins, but we have to say just The Boss nowadays.'

   Further on, where in RK (p. 279) it is said that 'The new "Chief" evidently had means of getting news', A has 'the New Mayor [?or] Chief Shirriff'; but this was changed to 'the Boss or Chief Shirriff'. When 'arrested' at Frogmorton Frodo and his companions are told that 'It's [Mayor's >] the Chief Shirriff's orders', where RK (p. 280) has 'It's the Chief's orders'.

2 But see p. 111.

3 The village was named *Frogbarn*, with *Frogmorton* written above as an alternative (and *Frogmorton* occurs in the text subsequently); and the date of their ride from the Brandywine Bridge was 'the fifth of November in the Shire-reckoning', with '1st' (the date in RK) written above. The village was 'about 25 miles from the Bridge' ('about twenty-two miles' in RK).

4 The name *Smallburrow* was written so, as in RK, at the first occurrence, but thereafter *Smallburrows*.

5 'Shire-house' is used in A for 'Shirriff-house' in RK. Sam asks what the term means, and Robin Smallburrows replies: 'Well, you ought to know, Sam. You were in one last night, and didn't find it to your liking, we hear.'

6 See p. 95.

7 The text here is very difficult. Above '(I told) the Boss' my father first wrote 'Long Tom' before changing this to 'Big Sharkey'. The end of the ruffian's remarks as first written cannot be read: 'but the Boss says no, and [?Long Tom] ..... way' (just possibly 'goes his way').

8 There is a note on the manuscript here which is partly illegible: ' .... only Cosimo .... What happened to Otho?' In 'Three is Company' (*The Fellowship of the Ring* p. 75) it is said that Otho Sackville-Baggins 'had died some years before, at the ripe but disappointed age of 102', and this goes back to an early stage.

9 See the note given on p. 77 ('Gandalf should stay at Bree ...').

10   In RK Farmer Cotton is named Tom.

11   Sting had been given to Sam by Frodo in 'The Land of Shadow'
(p. 32; RK p. 204); but Frodo wields Sting in his combat at Bag
End with the chief of the orc-men (p. 92). In a passage that was
introduced in the Second Edition Frodo was induced to receive it
back at the Field of Cormallen (see p. 50).

12   *the Road Bend*: the westward turn in the road to Hobbiton at
Bywater Pool. On the large-scale map of the Shire that I made in
1943 (VI.107) the bend is more marked and more nearly a right
angle than it is on the small map in *The Fellowship of the Ring*.

13   *October* is a slip for *November*: see note 3.

14   By 'There's no way from the West' Farmer Cotton meant, I
suppose, that there was no other way back from Michel Delving
but by taking the East Road, since the ruffians could not or would
not pass through the Tookland.

15   There are a couple of pages of roughly pencilled text which
repeat, with minor alterations and extensions, this section of the
chapter in A, made perhaps because my father recognised the
near-illegibility of the original, and these pages have provided
help in elucidating it here and there (characteristically, the words
or phrases that defy elucidation in the original text are expressed
differently in the second). At this point the pencilled text has:
'They've caught a ruffian or two and thrashed 'em in the Tookus'
(*Tookus* < *Took-house*, as *workhouse* became *workus*).

16   I do not know whether *the Long Smial* is to be equated with *the
Took-house*. – This is the first appearance of the word *smial*,
which seems clearly to be written thus, although in the second
text of 'The Scouring of the Shire' it is written *Smiles* (see p. 99
and note 28). Since Pippin was born in the Long Smial, it must be
the forerunner of the Great Smials. These were at Tuckborough
(Pippin speaks in Fangorn Forest of 'the Great Place of the Tooks
away back in the Smials at Tuckborough', TT p. 64), but the
name as written here is not in fact *Tuckborough*: it looks more
like *Tuckbery* (not *Tuckbury*). However, there are many words
wrongly written in this manuscript (in the next line of the text,
for instance, the word I have given as '[?stout]' can really only be
interpreted as 'stood').

17   The text could conceivably be interpreted as 'he had the block on
the East [Road] strengthened', although no road-block on the
East Road has been mentioned. The second, pencilled text of this
part of the chapter (see note 15) has here: 'He had a block made
on the Road at the waymeet.' This text gives out a few lines
beyond this point.

18   It is interesting to look back at early references to the destruction
in the Shire. In a note probably belonging to the time of the
outline 'The Story Foreseen from Moria' (VII.216) my father

wrote: 'Cosimo has industrialised it. Factories and smoke. The Sandymans have a biscuit factory. Iron is found'; and in the earliest reference to the Mirror in Lothlórien Frodo was to see 'Trees being felled and a tall building being made where the old mill was. Gaffer Gamgee turned out. Open trouble, almost war, between Marish and Buckland on one hand – and the West. Cosimo Sackville-Baggins very rich, buying up land' (VII.249; cf. also VII.253, where there is a reference to the tall chimney being built on the site of the old mill).

In 'The old farm on the right' one should possibly read 'left' for 'right'; cf. my father's painting of Hobbiton, and the words of the final text of 'The Scouring of the Shire' (RK p. 296): 'The Old Grange on the west side had been knocked down, and its place taken by rows of tarred sheds.'

19   Later in this manuscript (p. 108) the Tree in the Party Field had been cut down and burned.

20   The reference is to 'The Shadow of the Past' (FR p. 71): 'I feel that as long as the Shire lies behind, safe and comfortable, I shall find wandering more bearable: I shall know that somewhere there is a firm foothold, even if my feet cannot stand there again.'

21   *I am told you sleep sound:* cf. the words of the orc-man at Bywater, speaking of Cosimo (an addition to the text, p. 83): 'He sleeps sound, and I shouldn't try and wake him now.'

22   Earlier in this narrative Sam wielded Sting: p. 86 and note 11.

23   At the top of the page on which Frodo's words appear my father wrote: 'Ah, and you said in Mordor you'd never strike another blow,' said Sam. 'Just shows you never know.' See p. 80.

24   *Waymoot*: *Waymeet* in RK. My original large-scale map of the Shire made in 1943 (VI.107) has *Waymoot*, as also that published in *The Fellowship of the Ring*; but the second manuscript of 'The Scouring of the Shire' has *Waymeet*. Presumably my father changed his mind about the form but neglected the map.

25   It is not explained how Frodo knew that this person, when he met him at Bag End, was called 'Sharkey'.

26   Cf. Saruman's words at the end of the chapter (p. 102): 'I believe all my men used to call me that in the better times. They were so devoted' (RK: 'All my people used to call me that in Isengard, I believe. A sign of affection, possibly'). The footnote to the text in RK p. 298 'It was probably Orkish in origin: *Sharkū* [Second Edition *Sharkû*], "old man"' was not added until the book was in page proof.

27   A rewritten account of the arrest at Frogmorton and Sam's conversation with Robin Smallburrow was inserted into manuscript B. This is almost as in RK, but as first written Robin's reply to Sam's question 'So that's how the news of us reached you, was it?' was different:

'Not directly. A message came down from the Chief at Bag End, about two hours ago, that you were to be arrested. I reckon someone must have slipped down from the Bridge to Stock, where there's a small gang of his Men. Someone went through Frogmorton on a big horse last night.'

This was changed at once to the text of RK (p. 282), but with 'One [runner] came in from Bamfurlong last night'. *Bamfurlong* was the reading of the First Edition here. In the Second Edition it was changed to *Whitfurrows* (which though shown on the map of the Shire was never mentioned in the text of the First Edition), and the name *Bamfurlong* was given to Maggot's farm in 'A Short Cut to Mushrooms' (FR p. 100): 'We are on old Farmer Maggot's land' of the First Edition became 'This is Bamfurlong; old Farmer Maggot's land.'

28   Cf. *the Long Smial* in A (note 16). A draft for the present passage has: 'those deep places the Old Smiles in the Green Hills'. I would guess that my father introduced *Smiles* as being the most natural spelling if the old word had survived into Modern English, but then abandoned it (it was changed to *Smials* on the B text) as being capable of an absurd interpretation. Cf. Appendix F (II, 'On Translation'): '*smial* (or *smile*) "burrow" is a likely form for a descendant of *smygel*'.

29   This rider was inserted at a late stage, for as in RK Merry interrupts Farmer Cotton with a question ('Who is this Sharkey?'); thus he was no longer away in Tuckborough with Pippin, but had assumed his rôle as commander of the operations at Bywater.

30   The only differences worth noting are that the trees had been felled along the Bywater Road 'for fuel for the engine'; and that a few men were still present in the huts at Hobbiton, who 'when they saw the force that approached fled away over the fields.'

31   It is said in the Prologue to *The Lord of the Rings* that 'before this story opens' 'the only [battle] that had ever been fought within the borders of the Shire was beyond living memory: the Battle of Greenfields, S.R.1147, in which Bandobras Took routed an invasion of Orcs.' The date 1137 was corrected to 1147 on the text C. – See p. 119.

32   In the First Edition the meeting with Saruman took place after the company had left Dunland: see p. 69.

X

THE GREY HAVENS

The original writing down of the last chapter of *The Lord of the Rings* was the continuation of the long uninterrupted draft text ('A') that extends back through 'The Scouring of the Shire' and 'Homeward Bound' (see pp. 75, 79), and which I left at the end of the Battle of Bywater on p. 93. That text continues:

> And so the year drew to its end. Even Sam could find no fault with Frodo's fame and honour in his own country. The Tooks were too secure in their traditional position – and after all their folkland was the only one that had never given in to the ruffians – and also too generous to be really jealous; yet it was plain that the name of Baggins would become the most famous in Hobbit-history.

From this point the text of A, rough but now fully legible, differs chiefly from the final form of the chapter not in what is actually told nor in how it is told but in the absence of several significant features and a good deal of detail that were added in later. For example, while the rescue of Lobelia Sackville-Baggins from the Lockholes in Michel Delving and the disposition of her property is told much as in RK, there is no mention of Fredegar Bolger; and nothing is said of the hunting out of the gangs of men in the south of the Shire by Merry and Pippin. Frodo became the Mayor, not the Deputy Mayor, although the difference was only one of title, since he made it a condition of his acceptance that Will Whitfoot should become Mayor again 'as soon as the mess is cleared up'; and his inactivity in the office is not mentioned. As my father first set it down the account in RK (pp. 302–4) of the work of restoration and repair, of Sam's planting of young trees, of the fruitfulness of the year 1420,[1] and of Sam's marriage to Rose Cotton was very largely reached. In this text there is no reference to 'Sharkey's Men', and the jocular name given in Bywater to the restored Bagshot Row was 'Ruffians' End'. The seed in Galadriel's box is described as 'like a nut or a dried berry', its colour golden-yellow; Sam planted it in the Party Field 'where the tree had been burned' (see p. 90).

There is in A no reference to Frodo's first illness in March of 1420, when in Sam's absence Farmer Cotton found him on his bed 'clutching a white gem that hung on a chain about his neck' (the gift of Arwen recorded in 'Many Partings'). The passage in RK (p. 305) describing the finery and magnificence of Merry and Pippin, in contrast to the 'ordinary attire' of Frodo and Sam, is lacking, and so the further reference to the white jewel that Frodo always wore is also absent. Since my father had written a couple of pages earlier that 'Even Sam could find no fault with Frodo's fame and honour in his own country', the sharply contrasting picture in RK is of course lacking: 'Frodo dropped quietly out of all the doings of the Shire, and Sam was pained to notice how little honour he had in his own country. Few people knew or wanted to know about his deeds and adventures ...'

Frodo's illness on the sixth of October 1420, the date of the attack of the Ringwraiths at Weathertop two years before, is recorded, but not that in March 1421. The naming of Sam's eldest daughter *Elanor* ('born on 25 March as Sam duly noted') on Frodo's suggestion is told, and the big book with red leather covers is described, without however any mention of the title page and the sequence of Bilbo's rejected titles; the writing in the book ended at Chapter 77 (the number being marked with a query).[2]

The last part of the chapter was set down with great sureness, though not all elements in the final story were immediately present. At the meeting of Frodo and Sam with the Elves in the Woody End there is no mention of the Great Rings of Elrond and Galadriel;[3] at Mithlond Círdan the Shipwright does not appear (but enters in a later marginal addition), nor is Gandalf said to bear the Third Ring; and Frodo's sight of the 'far green country under a swift sunrise' is absent (though this also is roughed in marginally; the linking of Frodo's passage over the Sea 'with the vision he had of a far green country in the house of Tom Bombadil' had been referred to in my father's letter of November 1944, see p. 53). I give here the text of A from the coming of the company to Mithlond:

And when they had passed the Shire by the south skirts of the White Downs they came to the Far Downs and the Towers and looked on the Sea; and rode down at last to Mithlond the Grey Havens in the long firth of Lūne. And there was a ship lying at the haven, and upon the quays stood one robed also in white. It was Gandalf, and he welcomed them; and they were glad for then they knew that he also would take ship with them.

But Sam was now sad at heart, and it seemed to him that if the parting would be bitter, even worse would be the lonely ride home. But even as they stood there and were ready to go aboard, up rode Merry and Pippin in great haste. And amid his tears Pippin laughed. 'You tried to give us the slip once before and failed, Frodo, and this time you have nearly done it, but you've failed again.' 'It was not Sam this time who gave you away,' said Merry, 'but Gandalf himself.'

'Yes,' said Gandalf. 'It will be better to ride back three together than one alone. Well, here at last, dear friends, on the shores of the Sea comes an end of our fellowship in Middle-earth. Go in peace; and I will not say, do not weep, for not all tears are an evil.'

Then Frodo kissed Merry and Pippin and last of all Sam, and went aboard, and the sails were drawn up, and the wind blew, and slowly the ship sailed away down the [?pale] Gulf of Lune. And it was night again; and Sam looked on the grey sea and saw a shadow on the waters that was lost in the West. And he stood a while hearing the sigh and murmur of the waves on the shores of Middle-earth, and the sound of it remained in his heart for ever, though he never spoke of it. And Merry and Pippin stood silent beside him.

The long ride back to the Shire is told in almost the same words as in *The Return of the King*. And thus the Third Age was brought to its final end, in this most memorable of partings, without hesitation and with assured simplicity; the unmistakeable voices of Merry and Pippin, the still more unmistakeable voice of Gandalf in his last words on Middle-earth, and the beginning of the voyage that was bearing away into the True West the hobbits, Bilbo and Frodo, leaving Sam behind.

A manuscript of the chapter as a separate entity ('B') followed, subsequently numbered 'LX' and entitled 'The Grey Havens'. It was written before the changed view of Frodo's reputation in the Shire had entered, but with emendations and additions it reached the final form in almost all the features in which A differed from it. My father did not yet realise, however, that Fredegar Bolger languished in the Lockholes along with Will Whitfoot and Lobelia Sackville-Baggins; and of Lobelia it was said in a first draft of the passage concerning her that 'She never got over the news of poor Cosimo's murder, and she said that it was not his fault; he was led astray by that wicked Sharkey and never meant any harm.'

Frodo's first illness was still absent as B was originally written, and when it was introduced it was in these words:

Sam was away on his forestry work in March, and Frodo was glad, for he had been feeling ill, and it would have been difficult to conceal from Sam. On the twelfth of March[4] he was in pain and weighed down with a great sense of darkness, and could do little more than walk about clasping the jewel of Queen Arwen. But after a while the fit passed.

An idea that was never carried further appears in a hastily scribbled passage on this manuscript, apparently intended for inclusion before 'Little Elanor was nearly six months old, and 1421 had passed to its autumn' (RK p. 306):

At midsummer Gandalf appeared suddenly, and his visit was long remembered for the astonishing things that happened to all the bonfires (which hobbit [?children] light on midsummer's eve). The whole Shire was lit with lights of many colours until the dawn came, and it seemed that the fire [??ran wild for him] over all the land so that the grass was kindled with glittering jewels, and the trees were hung with red and gold blossom all through the night, and the Shire was full of light and song until the dawn came.

No other trace of this idea is found. Perhaps my father felt that when Gandalf declared that his time was over he meant no less.[5]

The title page of the Red Book of Westmarch first appears in B, with Bilbo's titles written one above the other and all struck through (which was the meaning of the word 'so' in 'crossed out one after another, so:', RK p. 307):

Memoirs of An Amateur Burglar
My Unexpected Journey
There and Back Again   and What Happened After
Adventures of Five Hobbits
The Case of the Great Ring (compiled from the records
     and notes of B. Baggins and others)
What the Bagginses Did in the War of the Ring
(here Bilbo's hand ended and Frodo had written:)
The
Downfall
of
The Lord of the Rings
and
The Return of the King
(as seen by B. and F. Baggins, S. Gamgee, M. Brandybuck, P. Took,
     supplemented by information provided by the Wise)

In the typescript that followed B the following was added:

Together with certain excerpts from Books of Lore
translated by B. Baggins in Rivendell[6]

In B appeared the Three Rings of the Elves on the fingers of their bearers, but they were not yet named. It was not until the book was in galley proof that 'Vilya, mightiest of the Three' was added to the description of Elrond's Ring, Gandalf's Ring was named 'Narya the

Great', and that of Galadriel became 'Nenya, the ring wrought of *mithril*'.

Lastly, both in A and in B my father set within square brackets, his usual sign of doubt, certain of Frodo's words to Sam in the Woody End, thus: 'No, Sam. Not yet anyway, not further than the Havens. [Though you too were a Ringbearer, if only for a little while: your time may come.]'

NOTES

1 Absent from the account of the year 1420 is the sentence in RK, p. 303: 'All the children born or begotten in that year, and there were many, were fair to see and strong, and most of them had a rich golden hair that had before been rare among hobbits.' This entered in the first typescript text. See p. 134, note 12.

2 In the following text the last, unfinished chapter in the Red Book was numbered '72', and on the first typescript this was changed to '80', as in RK.

3 The chant to Elbereth began thus:

> O Elbereth Gilthoniel
> Silivren pennar oriel!
> Gilthoniel O Elbereth ...

Cf. VI.394. This was repeated in the second text of the chapter, but *oriel* was emended to *íriel*. This in turn was repeated on the first typescript, and then the opening was changed to its form in RK:

> A! Elbereth Gilthoniel
> silivren penna míriel
> o menel aglar elenath ...

To Bilbo's question (RK p. 309) 'Are you coming?' Frodo replies here: 'Yes, I am coming, *before the wound returns*. And the Ringbearers should go together.' Frodo was speaking of the sickness that had come on him on October the sixth, the date of his wounding at Weathertop, in each of the following years. It was now 22 September (Bilbo's birthday); on the twenty-ninth of the month the ship sailed from the Grey Havens. On the third anniversary of the attack at Weathertop *The Lord of the Rings* ends, for it was on that day, according to *The Tale of Years*, that Sam returned to Bag End.

4 The date was corrected to the thirteenth of March on the following typescript text. This in the final chronology was the anniversary of the poisoning of Frodo by Shelob, as noted in *The Tale of Years*. Frodo's third illness, in the following year, also fell on March 13, according to *The Tale of Years*.

5 But he had perhaps intended that a final visit by Gandalf to the Shire should be recorded; as Gandalf said when he parted from the

hobbits in the note on the draft manuscript of 'Homeward Bound' (p. 77): 'I'll be along some time.'

6 In the two typescript texts of the chapter the crossings-out were omitted, and Bilbo's first title 'Memoirs of an Amateur Burglar' was replaced by 'My Diary'. 'What Happened After' was still shown as an addition, and the words 'and friends' were added after 'Bagginses' in Bilbo's final title; in the margins of both typescripts my father noted that the corrections were to be printed as such, representing the original title-page. The final form of the page was introduced on the galley proof.

XI

THE EPILOGUE

The words that end *The Lord of the Rings*, ' "Well, I'm back," he said', were not intended to do so when my father wrote them in the long draft manuscript A which has been followed in the previous chapters. It is obvious from the manuscript that the text continued on without break;[1] and there is in fact no indication that my father thought of what he was writing as markedly separate from what preceded. I give now this last part of A: very rough, but legible throughout. The ages of Sam's children were added, almost certainly at the time of writing: Elanor 15, Frodo 13, Rose 11, Merry 9, Pippin 7.

And one evening in March [*added:* 1436][2] Master Samwise Gamgee was taking his ease by a fire in his study, and the children were all gathered about him, as was not at all unusual, though it was always supposed to be a special treat.

He had been reading aloud (as was usual) from a big Red Book on a stand, and on a stool beside him sat Elanor, and she was a beautiful child more fair-skinned than most hobbit-maids and more slender, and she was now running up into her 'teens; and there was Frodo-lad on the heathrug, in spite of his name as good a copy of Sam as you could wish, and Rose, Merry, and Pippin were sitting in chairs much too big for them. Goldilocks had gone to bed, for in this Frodo's foretelling had made a slight error and she came after Pippin, and was still only five and the Red Book rather too much for her yet. But she was not the last of the line, for Sam and Rose seemed likely to rival old Gerontius Took in the number of their children as successfully as Bilbo had passed his age. There was little Ham, and there was Daisie in her cradle.

'Well dear,' said Sam, 'it grew there once, because I saw it with my own eyes.'

'Does it grow there still, daddy?'

'I don't see why it shouldn't, Ellie. I've never been on my travels again, as you know, having all you young folk to mind –

regular ragtag and bobtail old Saruman would have called it. But Mr. Merry and Mr. Pippin, they've been south more than once, for they sort of belong there too now.'

'And haven't they grown big?' said Merry. 'I wish I could grow big like Mr. Meriadoc of Buckland. He's the biggest hobbit that ever was: bigger than Bandobras.'

'Not bigger than Mr. Peregrin of Tuckborough,' said Pippin, 'and he's got hair that's almost golden. Is he Prince Peregrin away down in the Stone City, dad?'

'Well, he's never said so,' said Sam, 'but he's highly thought of, that I know. But now where were [we] getting to?'

'Nowhere,' said Frodo-lad. 'I want to hear about the Spider again. I like the parts best where you come in, dad.'

'But dad, you were talking about Lórien,' said Elanor, 'and whether my flower still grows there.'

'I expect it does, Ellie dear. For as I was saying, Mr. Merry, he says that though the Lady has gone the Elves still live there.'

'When can I go and see? I want to see Elves, dad, and I want to see my own flower.'

'If you look in a glass you'll see one that is sweeter,' said Sam, 'though I should not be telling you, for you'll find it out soon enough for yourself.'

'But that isn't the same. I want to see the green hill and the white flowers and the golden and hear the Elves sing.'

'Then maybe you will one day,' said Sam. 'I said the same when I was your age, and long after, and there didn't seem no hope, and yet it came true.'

'But the Elves are sailing away still, aren't they, and soon there'll be none, will there, dad?' said Rose; 'and then all will be just places, and very nice, but, but ...'

'But what, Rosie-lass?'

'But not like in stories.'

'Well, it would be so if they all was to sail,' said Sam. 'But I am told they aren't sailing any more. The Ring has left the Havens, and those that made up their mind to stay when Master Elrond left are staying. And so there'll be Elves still for many and many a day.'

'Still I think it was very sad when Master Elrond left Rivendell and the Lady left Lórien,' said Elanor. 'What happened to Celeborn? Is he very sad?'

'I expect so, dear. Elves are sad; and that's what makes them so beautiful, and why we can't see much of them. He lives in his own land as he always has done,' said Sam. 'Lórien is his land, and he loves trees.'

'No one else in the world hasn't got a Mallorn like we have, have they?' said Merry. 'Only us and Lord Keleborn.'[3]

'So I believe,' said Sam. Secretly it was one of the greatest prides of his life. 'Well, Keleborn lives among the Trees, and he is happy in his Elvish way, I don't doubt. They can afford to wait, Elves can. His time is not come yet. The Lady came to his land and now she is gone;[4] and he has the land still. When he tires of it he can leave it. So with Legolas, he came with his people and they live in the land across the River, Ithilien, if you can say that, and they've made it very lovely, according to Mr. Pippin. But he'll go to Sea one day, I don't doubt. But not while Gimli's still alive.'

'What's happened to Gimli?' said Frodo-lad. 'I liked him. Please can I have an axe soon, dad? Are there any orcs left?'

'I daresay there are if you know where to look,' said Sam. 'But not in the Shire, and you won't have an axe for chopping off heads, Frodo-lad. We don't make them. But Gimli, he came down to work for the King in the City, and he and his folk worked so long they got used to it and proud of their work, and in the end they settled up in the mountains up away west behind the City, and there they are still. And Gimli goes once every other year to see the Glittering Caves.'

'And does Legolas go to see Treebeard?' asked Elanor.

'I can't say, dear,' said Sam. 'I've never heard of anyone as has ever seen an Ent since those days. If Mr. Merry or Mr. Pippin have they keep it secret. Very close are Ents.'

'And have they never found the Entwives?'

'Well, we've seen none here, have we?' said Sam.

'No,' said Rosie-lass; 'but I look for them when I go in a wood. I would like the Entwives to be found.'

'So would I,' said Sam, 'but I'm afraid that is an old trouble, too old and too deep for folks like us to mend, my dear. But now no more questions tonight, at least not till after supper.'

'But that won't be fair,' said both Merry and Pippin, who were not in their teens. 'We shall have to go directly to bed.'

'Don't talk like that to me,' said Sam sternly. 'If it ain't fair for Ellie and Fro to sit up after supper it ain't fair for them to be born sooner, and it ain't fair that I'm your dad and you're not mine. So no more of that, take your turn and what's due in your time, or I'll tell the King.'

They had heard this threat before, but something in Sam's voice made it sound more serious on this occasion. 'When will you see the King?' said Frodo-lad.

'Sooner than you think,' said Sam. 'Well now, let's be fair. I'll tell you all, stay-uppers and go-to-bedders, a big secret. But don't you go whispering and waking up the youngsters. Keep it till tomorrow.'

A dead hush of expectancy fell on all the children: they watched him as hobbit-children of other times had watched the wizard Gandalf.

'The King's coming here,' said Sam solemnly.

'Coming to Bag End!' cried the children.

'No,' said Sam. 'But he's coming north. He won't come into the Shire because he has given orders that no Big Folk are to enter this land again after those Ruffians; and he will not come himself just to show he means it. But he will come to the Bridge. And —— ' Sam paused. 'He has issued a very special invitation to every one of you. Yes, by name!'

Sam went to a drawer and took out a large scroll. It was black and written in letters of silver.

'When did that come, dad?' said Merry.

'It came with the Southfarthing post three days ago [*written above:* on Wednesday],' said Elanor. 'I saw it. It was wrapped in silk and sealed with big seals.'

'Quite right, my bright eyes,' said Sam. 'Now look.' He unrolled it. 'It is written in Elvish and in Plain Language,' said Sam. 'And it says: *Elessar Aragorn Arathornsson the Elfstone King of Gondor and Lord of the Westlands will approach the Bridge of Baranduin on the first day of Spring, or in the Shire-reckoning the twenty-fifth day of March next, and desires there to greet all his friends. In especial he desires to see Master Samwise Mayor of the Shire, and Rose his wife, and Elanor, Rose, Goldilocks and Daisie his daughters, and Frodo, Merry, and Pippin and Hamfast his sons.* There you are, there are all your names.'

'But they aren't the same in both lists,' said Elanor, who could read.

'Ah,' said Sam, 'that's because the first list is Elvish. You're the same, Ellie, in both, because your name is Elvish; but Frodo is *Iorhail*, and Rose is *Beril*, and Merry is *Riben* [> *R..el* > *Gelir*], and Pippin is *Cordof*, and Goldilocks is *Glorfinniel*, and Hamfast is *Marthanc*, and Daisy [*so spelt*] is *Arien*. So now you know.'

'Well that's splendid,' said Frodo, 'now we all have Elvish names, but what is yours, dad?'

'Well, that's rather peculiar,' said Sam, 'for in the Elvish part, if you must know, what the King says is *Master Perhail who should rather be called Lanhail*, and that means, I believe, "Samwise or Halfwise who should rather be called Plain-wise". So now you know what the King thinks of your dad you'll maybe give more heed to what he says.'

'And ask him lots more questions,' said Frodo.

'When is March the 25th?' said Pippin, to whom days were still the longest measures of time that could really be grasped. 'Is it soon?'

'It's a week today,' said Elanor. 'When shall we start?'

'And what shall we wear?' said Rose.

'Ah,' said Sam. 'Mistress Rose will have a say in that. But you'll be surprised, my dears. We have had warning of this a long time and we've prepared for the day. You're going in the most lovely clothes you've ever seen, and we're riding in a coach. And if you're all very good and look as lovely as you do now I shouldn't be at all surprised if the King does not ask us to go with him to his house up by the Lake. And the Queen will be there.'

'And shall we stay up to supper?' said Rose, to whom the nearness of promotion made this an ever-present concern.

'We shall stay for weeks, until the hay-harvest at least,' said Sam. 'And we shall do what the King says. But as for staying up to supper, no doubt the Queen will have a word. And now if you haven't enough to whisper about for hours, and to dream about till the sun rises, then I don't know what more I can tell you.'

The stars were shining in a clear sky: it was the first day of the clear bright spell that came every year to the Shire at the end of March, and was every year welcomed and praised as something surprising for the time of the year.

All the children were in bed. Lights were glimmering still in Hobbiton and in many houses dotted about the darkening countryside. Sam stood at the door and looked away eastward. He drew Mistress Rose to him and held her close to his side. 'March 18th [> 25th]',[5] he said. 'This time seventeen years ago, Rose wife, I did not think I should ever see thee again. But I kept on hoping.'

['And I never hoped at all, Sam,' she said, 'until that very day; and then suddenly I did. In the middle of the morning I began singing, and father said "Quiet lass, or the Ruffians will come," and I said "Let them come. Their time will soon be over. My Sam's coming back." And he came.']⁶

'And you came back,' said Rose.

'I did,' said Sam; 'to the most belovedest place in all the world. I was torn in two then, lass, but now I am all whole. And all that I have, and all that I have had I still have.'

Here the text as it was written ends, but subsequently my father added to it the following:

They went in and shut the door. But even as he did so Sam heard suddenly the sigh and murmur of the sea on the shores of Middle-earth.

It cannot be doubted that this was how he intended at that time that *The Lord of the Rings* should end.

A fair copy ('B') followed, and this was headed 'Epilogue', without chapter-number; subsequently 'Epilogue' was altered to 'The End of the Book', again without number. The changes made to the original draft were remarkably few: very minor adjustments and improvements in the flow of the conversation between Sam and his children, and the alteration or enlargement of certain details.

Merry Gamgee now knows that Bandobras Took 'killed the goblin-king': the reference is to 'An Unexpected Party' in *The Hobbit*, where it is told that the Bullroarer 'charged the ranks of the goblins of Mount Gram in the Battle of the Green Fields, and knocked their king Golfimbul's head clean off with a wooden club.' Of the sailing of the Elves Sam now says, not that 'they aren't sailing any more', but that 'they are not sailing often now', and he continues: 'Those that stayed behind when Elrond left are mostly going to stay for good, or for a very long time. But they are more and more difficult to find or to talk to.' Of Ents he observes that they are 'very close, very secret-like, and they don't like people very much'; and of the Dwarves who came from Erebor to Minas Tirith with Gimli he says 'I hear they've settled up in the White Mountains not very far from the City', while 'Gimli goes once a year to see the Glittering Caves' (in Appendix A III, at end, it is said that Gimli 'became Lord of the Glittering Caves').

The King's letter now begins *Aragorn Arathornsson Elessar the Elfstone*; and the date of his coming to the Brandywine Bridge was now 'the eighth day of Spring, or in the Shire-reckoning the second of April', since my father had decided, already while writing A (see note 5), that the 25th of March was not the day on which the King would come to the Bridge, but the day on which *The Lord of the Rings* came to an end.[7]

Daisie Gamgee's name is now *Erien* (*Arien* in A); and in the King's letter he calls Sam *Master Perhail who should rather be called Panthail*, which Sam interprets as 'Master Samwise who ought to be called Fullwise'.

Other changes were made to B later, and these were taken up into the third and final text 'C' of this version of the 'Epilogue', a typescript. To this my father gave the revised title of B, 'The End of the Book', with a chapter-number 'LVIII',[8] but he then struck out both title and number and reverted to 'Epilogue.' The text now opens thus:

One evening in the March of 1436 Master Samwise Gamgee was taking his ease by the fire in his study, and his children were gathered round him, as was not at all unusual. Though it was always supposed to be a special occasion, a Royal Command, it was one more often commanded by the subjects than by the King.

This day, however, really was a special occasion. For one thing it was Elanor's birthday;[9] for another, Sam had been reading aloud from a big Red Book, and he had just come to the very end, after a slow progress through its many chapters that had taken many months. On a stool beside him sat Elanor ...

Sam now says of the Entwives: 'I think maybe the Entwives don't want to be found'; and after his words 'But now no more questions tonight' the following passage was introduced:

'Just one more, please!' begged Merry. 'I've wanted to ask before, but Ellie and Fro get in so many questions there's never any room for mine.'

'Well then, just one more,' said Sam.

'About horses,' said Merry. 'How many horses did the Riders lose in the battle, and have they grown lots more? And what happened to Legolas's horse? And what did Gandalf do with Shadowfax? And can I have a pony soon?' he ended breathlessly.

'That's a lot more than one question: you're worse than Gollum,' said Sam. 'You're going to have a pony next birthday, as I've told you before. Legolas let his horse run back free to Rohan from Isengard; and the Riders have more horses than ever, because nobody steals them any longer; and Shadowfax went in the White Ship with Gandalf: of course Gandalf couldn't have a' left him behind. Now that'll have to do. No more questions. At least not till after supper.'

The letter of the King now begins *Aragorn Tarantar* (at which Sam explains 'that's Trotter') *Aranthornsson* &c. *Tarantar* was altered on the typescript to *Telcontar* ('that's Strider'): see VIII.390 and note 14. Rose's name in Elvish becomes *Meril* (for *Beril*), and Hamfast's *Baravorn* (for *Marthanc*); the Elvish name of Daisy (so spelt in C) reverts to *Arien* (for *Erien*), the form in A.

Though never published, of course, this version of the Epilogue is, I believe, quite well known, from copies made from the text at Marquette University. My father would never in fact have published it, even had he decided in the end to conclude *The Lord of the Rings* with an epilogue, for it was superseded by a second version, in which while much of Sam's news from beyond the Shire was retained its framework and presentation were radically changed.[10] Of this there are two texts. The first is a good clear manuscript with few corrections; it has neither title nor chapter-number. The second is a typescript, which though made by my father followed the manuscript very closely indeed; this is entitled 'Epilogue', with the chapter-number 'X' (i.e. of Book Six). I give here the text of the typescript in full.

The second version of the Epilogue

EPILOGUE

One evening in the March of 1436 Master Samwise Gamgee was in his study at Bag End. He was sitting at the old well-worn desk, and with many pauses for thought he was writing in his slow round hand on sheets of loose paper. Propped up on a stand at his side was a large red book in manuscript.

Not long before he had been reading aloud from it to his family. For the day was a special one: the birthday of his daughter Elanor. That evening before supper he had come at last to the very end of the Book. The long progress through its many chapters, even with omissions that he had thought advisable, had taken some months, for he only read aloud on great days. At the birthday reading, besides Elanor, Frodo-lad had been present, and Rosie-lass, and young Merry and Pippin; but the other children had not been there. The Red Book was not for them yet, and they were safely in bed. Goldilocks was only five years old, for in this Frodo's foretelling had made a slight error, and she came after Pippin. But she was not the last of the line, for Samwise and Rose seemed likely to rival old Gerontius Took as successfully in the number of their children as Bilbo had in the number of his years. There was little Ham, [and there was Daisy still in her cradle >] and Daisy, and there was Primrose still in her cradle.[11]

Now Sam was 'having a bit of quiet'. Supper was over. Only Elanor was with him, still up because it was her birthday. She sat without a sound, staring at the fire, and now and again glancing at her father. She was a beautiful girl, more fair of skin than most hobbit-maidens, and more slender, and the firelight glinted in her red-gold hair. To her, by gift if not by inheritance, a memory of elven-grace had descended.[12]

'What are you doing, Sam-dad[13] dear?' she said at last. 'You said you were going to rest, and I hoped you would talk to me.'

'Just a moment, Elanorellë,' said Sam,[14] as she came and set her arms about him and peered over his shoulder.

'It looks like Questions and Answers,' she said.

'And so it is,' said Sam. 'Mr. Frodo, he left the last pages of the Book to me, but I have never yet durst to put hand to them. I am still making notes, as old Mr. Bilbo would have said. Here's all the many questions Mother Rose and you and the children have asked, and I am writing out the answers, when I know them. Most of the questions are yours, because only you has heard all the Book more than once.'

'Three times,' said Elanor, looking at the carefully written page that lay under Sam's hand.

Q. *Dwarves, &c.* Frodo-lad says he likes them best. What happened to Gimli? Have the Mines of Moria been opened again? Are there any Orcs left?

A. *Gimli:* he came back to work for the King, as he said, and he brought many of his folk from the North, and they worked in Gondor so long that they got used to it, and they settled there, up in the White Mountains not far from the City. Gimli goes once a year to the Glittering Caves. How do I know? Information from Mr. Peregrin, who often goes back to Minas Tirith, where he is very highly thought of.

Moria: I have heard no news. Maybe the foretelling about Durin is not for our time.[15] Dark places still need a lot of cleaning up. I guess it will take a lot of trouble and daring deeds yet to root out the evil creatures from the halls of Moria. For there are certainly plenty of Orcs left in such places. It is not likely that we shall ever get quite rid of them.

Q. *Legolas.* Did he go back to the King? Will he stay there?

A. Yes, he did. He came south with Gimli, and he brought many of his people from Greenwood the Great (so they call it now). They say it was a wonderful sight to see companies of Dwarves and Elves journeying together. The Elves have made the City, and the land where Prince Faramir lives, more beautiful than ever. Yes, Legolas will stay there, at any rate as long as Gimli does; but I think he will go to the Sea one day. Mr. Meriadoc told me all this, for he has visited the Lady Éowyn in her white house.

Q. *Horses.* Merry is interested in these; very anxious for a pony of his own. How many horses did the Riders lose in the battles, and have they got some more now? What happened to Legolas's horse? What did Gandalf do with Shadowfax?

A. *Shadowfax* went in the White Ship with Gandalf, of course. I saw that myself. I also saw Legolas let his horse run free back to Rohan from Isengard. Mr. Meriadoc says he does not know how many horses were lost; but there are more than ever in Rohan now, because no one steals them any longer. The Riders also have many ponies, especially in Harrowdale: white, brown, and grey. Next year when he comes back from a visit to King Éomer he means to bring one for his namesake.

Q. *Ents.* Elanor would like to hear more about them. What did Legolas see in Fangorn; and does he ever see Treebeard now? Rosie-lass very anxious about Entwives. She looks for them whenever she goes in a wood. Will they ever be found? She would like them to be.

A. Legolas and Gimli have not told what they saw, so far as I have heard. I have not heard of any one that has seen an Ent since those days. Ents are very secret, and they do not like people much, big or little. I should like the Entwives to be found, too; but I am afraid that trouble is too old and deep for Shire-folk to mend. I think, maybe, Entwives do not want to be found; and maybe Ents are now tired of looking.

'Well dear,' said Sam, 'this top page, this is only today's batch.' He sighed. 'It isn't fit to go in the Book like that. It isn't a bit like the story as Mr. Frodo wrote it. But I shall have to make a chapter or two in proper style, somehow. Mr. Meriadoc might help me. He's clever at writing, and he's making a splendid book all about plants.'

'Don't write any more tonight. Talk to me, Sam-dad!' said Elanor, and drew him to a seat by the fire.

'Tell me,' she said, as they sat close together with the soft golden light on their faces, 'tell me about Lórien. Does *my* flower grow there still, Sam-dad?'

'Well dear, Celeborn still lives there among his trees and his Elves, and there I don't doubt your flower grows still. Though now I have got you to look at, I don't hanker after it so much.'

'But I don't want to look at myself, Sam-dad. I want to look at other things. I want to see the hill of Amroth where the King met Arwen, and the silver trees, and the little white niphredil, and the golden elanor in the grass that is always green. And I want to hear Elves singing.'

'Then, maybe, you will one day, Elanor. I said the same when I was your age, and long after it, and there didn't seem to be no hope. And yet I saw them, and I heard them.'

'I was afraid they were all sailing away, Sam-dad. Then soon there would be none here; and then everywhere would be just places, and'

'And what, Elanorellë?'

'And the light would have faded.'

'I know,' said Sam. 'The light is fading, Elanorellë. But it won't go out yet. It won't ever go quite out, I think now, since I have had you to talk to. For it seems to me now that people can remember it who have never seen it. And yet,' he sighed, 'even that is not the same as really seeing it, like I did.'

'Like really being in a story?' said Elanor. 'A story is quite different, even when it is about what happened. I wish I could go back to old days!'

'Folk of our sort often wish that,' said Sam. 'You came at the end of a great Age, Elanorellë; but though it's over, as we say, things don't really end sharp like that. It's more like a winter sunset. The High Elves have nearly all gone now with Elrond. But not quite all; and those that didn't go will wait now for a while. And the others, the ones that belong here, will last even longer. There are still things for you to see, and maybe you'll see them sooner than you hope.'

Elanor was silent for some time before she spoke again. 'I did not understand at first what Celeborn meant when he said

goodbye to the King,' she said. 'But I think I do now. He knew
that Lady Arwen would stay, but that Galadriel would leave
him.[16] I think it was very sad for him. And for you, dear
Sam-dad.' Her hand felt for his, and his brown hand clasped her
slender fingers. 'For your treasure went too. I am glad Frodo of
the Ring saw me, but I wish I could remember seeing him.'

'It was sad, Elanorellë,' said Sam, kissing her hair. 'It was, but
[it] isn't now. For why? Well, for one thing, Mr. Frodo has gone
where the elven-light isn't fading; and he deserved his reward.
But I have had mine, too. I have had lots of treasures. I am a
very rich hobbit. And there is one other reason, which I shall
whisper to you, a secret I have never told before to no one, nor
put in the Book yet. Before he went Mr. Frodo said that my time
maybe would come. I can wait. I think maybe we haven't said
farewell for good. But I can wait. I have learned that much from
the Elves at any rate. They are not so troubled about time. And
so I think Celeborn is still happy among his trees, in an Elvish
way. His time hasn't come, and he isn't tired of his land yet.
When he is tired he can go.'

'And when you're tired, you will go, Sam-dad. You will go to
the Havens with the Elves. Then I shall go with you. I shall not
part with you, like Arwen did with Elrond.'

'Maybe, maybe,' said Sam kissing her gently. 'And maybe
not. The choice of Lúthien and Arwen comes to many,
Elanorellë, or something like it; and it isn't wise to choose
before the time.

'And now, my dearest, I think that it's time even a lass of
fifteen spring-times should go to her bed. And I have words to
say to Mother Rose.'

Elanor stood up, and passed her hand lightly through Sam's
curling brown hair, already flecked with grey. 'Good night,
Sam-dad. But'

'I don't want *good night but*,' said Sam.

'But won't you show it me first? I was going to say.'

'Show you what, dear?'

'The King's letter, of course. You have had it now more than
a week.'

Sam sat up. 'Good gracious!' he said. 'How stories do repeat
themselves! And you get paid back in your own coin and all.
How we spied on poor Mr. Frodo! And now our own spy on us,
meaning no more harm than we did, I hope. But how do you
know about it?'

'There was no need for spying,' said Elanor. 'If you wanted it kept secret, you were not nearly careful enough. It came by the Southfarthing post early on Wednesday last week. I saw you take it in. All wrapped in white silk and sealed with great black seals: any one who had heard the Book would have guessed at once that it came from the King. Is it good news? Won't you show it me, Sam-dad?'

'Well, as you're so deep in, you'd better be right in,' said Sam. 'But no conspiracies now. If I show you, you join the grown-ups' side and must play fair. I'll tell the others in my own time. The King is coming.'

'He's coming here?' Elanor cried. 'To Bag End?'

'No, dear,' said Sam. 'But he's coming north again, as he hasn't done since you was a mite.[17] But now his house is ready. He won't come into the Shire, because he's given orders that no Big Folk are to enter the land again after those Ruffians, and he won't break his own rules. But he will ride to the Bridge. And he's sent a very special invitation to every one of us, every one by name.'

Sam went to a drawer, unlocked it, and took out a scroll, and slipped off its case. It was written in two columns with fair silver letters upon black. He unrolled it, and set a candle beside it on the desk, so that Elanor could see it.

'How splendid!' she cried. 'I can read the Plain Language, but what does the other side say? I think it is Elvish, but you've taught me so few Elvish words yet.'

'Yes, it's written in a kind of Elvish that the great folk of Gondor use,' said Sam. 'I have made it out, enough at least to be sure that it says much the same, only it turns all our names into Elvish. Yours is the same on both sides, Elanor, because your name *is* Elvish. But Frodo is *Iorhael*, and Rose is *Meril*, and Merry is *Gelir*, and Pippin is *Cordof*, and Goldilocks is *Glorfinniel*, and Hamfast is *Baravorn*, and Daisy is *Eirien*. So now you know.'

'How wonderful!' she said. 'Now we have all got Elvish names. What a splendid end to my birthday! But what is your name, Sam-dad? You didn't mention it.'

'Well, it's rather peculiar,' said Sam. 'For in the Elvish part, if you must know, the King says: "Master *Perhael* who should be called *Panthael*". And that means: Samwise who ought to be called Fullwise. So now you know what the King thinks of your old father.'

'Not a bit more than I do, Sam-dad, *Perhael-adar*[18] dearest,' said Elanor. 'But it says the second of April, only a week today![19] When shall we start? We ought to be getting ready. What shall we wear?'

'You must ask Mother Rose about all that,' said Sam. 'But we *have* been getting ready. We had a warning of this a long time ago; and we've said naught about it, only because we didn't want you all to lose your sleep of nights, not just yet. You have all got to look your best and beautifullest. You will all have beautiful clothes, and we shall drive in a coach.'

'Shall I make three curtsies, or only one?' said Elanor.

'One will do, one each for the King and the Queen,' said Sam. 'For though it doesn't say so in the letter, Elanorellë, I think the Queen will be there. And when you've seen her, my dear, you'll know what a lady of the Elves looks like, save that none are so beautiful. And there's more to it even than that. For I shall be surprised if the King doesn't bid us to his great house by Lake Evendim. And there will be Elladan and Elrohir, who still live in Rivendell – and with them will be Elves, Elanorellë, and they will sing by the water in the twilight. That is why I said you might see them sooner than you guessed.'

Elanor said nothing, but stood looking at the fire, and her eyes shone like stars. At last she sighed and stirred. 'How long shall we stay?' she asked. 'I suppose we shall have to come back?'

'Yes, and we shall want to, in a way,' said Sam. 'But we might stay until hay-harvest, when I must be back here. Good night, Elanorellë. Sleep now till the sun rises. You'll have no need of dreams.'

'Good night, Sam-dad. And don't work any more. For I know what your chapter should be. Write down our talk together – but not to-night.' She kissed him, and passed out of the room; and it seemed to Sam that the fire burned low at her going.

The stars were shining in a clear dark sky. It was the second day of the bright and cloudless spell that came every year to the Shire towards the end of March, and was every year welcomed and praised as something surprising for the season. All the children were now in bed. It was late, but here and there lights were still glimmering in Hobbiton, and in houses dotted about the night-folded countryside.

Master Samwise stood at the door and looked away eastward. He drew Mistress Rose to him, and set his arm about her.

'March the twenty-fifth!' he said. 'This day seventeen years
ago, Rose wife, I didn't think I should ever see thee again. But I
kept on hoping.'

'I never hoped at all, Sam,' she said, 'not until that very day;
and then suddenly I did. About noon it was, and I felt so glad
that I began singing. And mother said: "Quiet, lass! There's
ruffians about." And I said: "Let them come! Their time will
soon be over. Sam's coming back." And you came.'

'I did,' said Sam. 'To the most belovedest place in all the
world. To my Rose and my garden.'

They went in, and Sam shut the door. But even as he did so, he
heard suddenly, deep and unstilled, the sigh and murmur of the
Sea upon the shores of Middle-earth.

★

In this second Epilogue Sam does not read out the King's letter
(since Elanor could read), but associated with it (as is seen from the
name-forms *Eirien*, *Perhael*, *Panthael*) are three 'facsimiles' of the
letter, written in *tengwar* in two columns.

The first of these ('I') is reproduced on p. 130. It is accompanied by
a transliteration into 'plain letters' of both the English and the
Sindarin. The transliteration of the English does not precisely corres-
pond to the *tengwar* text, for the former omits *Arathornsson*, and
adds *day* where the *tengwar* text has 'the thirty-first of the Stirring'.
The words *and Arnor*, *ar Arnor* were added in to both the *tengwar*
texts and are lacking in the transliterations. As my father wrote them
they read as follows:

Aragorn Strider The Elfstone, King of Gondor and Lord of
the Westlands, will approach the Bridge of Baranduin on the
eighth day of Spring, or in the Shire-reckoning the second
day of April. And he desires to greet there all his friends.
In especial he desires to see Master *Samwise*, Mayor of the
Shire, and *Rose* his wife; and *Elanor*, *Rose*, *Goldilocks*, and
Daisy his daughters; and *Frodo*, *Merry*, *Pippin* and *Hamfast*
  his sons.

To Samwise and Rose the King's greeting from Minas
Tirith, the thirty-first day of the Stirring, being
the twenty-third of February in their reckoning.
A · E ·

Elessar Telcontar: Aragorn Arathornion Edhelharn, aran

Gondor ar Hîr i Mbair Annui, anglennatha i Varanduiniant
erin dolothen Ethuil, egor ben genediad Drannail erin
Gwirith edwen. Ar e aníra ennas suilannad mhellyn în
phain: *edregol* e aníra tírad i Cherdir *Perhael* (i sennui
Panthael estathar aen) Condir i Drann, ar *Meril* bess dîn,
ar *Elanor, Meril, Glorfinniel*, ar *Eirien* sellath dîn; ar
Iorhael, Gelir, Cordof, ar *Baravorn*, ionnath dîn.
    A *Pherhael* ar am *Meril* suilad uin aran o Minas
Tirith nelchaenen uin Echuir.
                                        A · E ·

The change of pen after *ar Elanor* was no doubt made in order to fit
the Sindarin text onto the page.
    The second 'facsimile' ('II'), not accompanied by a transliteration
and not reproduced here, is very similar to I, but *and Arnor, ar Arnor*
is part of the texts as written, there is no variation in the boldness of
the lettering, and the texts end at the words *his sons, ionnath dîn*,
followed by the initials A · E ·, so that there is here no mention of the
date and place of the letter.
    The third of these pages ('III'), preserved with the typescript text of
the second Epilogue and accompanied by a transliteration, is reproduced on p. 131. In this case the use of vowel-*tehtar* above conson-
nants in the Sindarin text greatly reduced its length. The English text is
the same as in I, but the note of the date is different: 'From Minas
Tirith, the twenty-third of February 6341' [= 1436]. The Sindarin text
differs from that of I and II in the word order:
    Aragorn Arathornion Edhelharn anglennatha iVaranduiniant
    erin dolothen Ethuil (egor ben genediad Drannail erin Gwirith
    edwen) ar ennas aníra i aran Gondor ar Arnor ar Hîr iMbair
    Annui [*written* Anui][20] suilannad mhellyn in phain ...
The note of date at the end of the Sindarin text reads:
    a Pherhael ar am Meril suilad uin aran o Minas Tirith
    nelchaenen ned Echuir: 61.[21]

It emerges from the account of his works that my father wrote for
Milton Waldman in 1951 that the second version of the Epilogue was
written at a very late stage. In this account he included what he called
'a long and yet bald résumé' of the story of *The Lord of the Rings*; this
was omitted in *Letters* (no. 131), and I give here its closing passages.

The 'Scouring of the Shire' ending in the last battle ever fought there
occupies a chapter. It is followed by a second spring, a marvellous
restoration and enhancement of beauty, chiefly wrought by Sam
(with the help of gifts given him in Lórien). But Frodo cannot be
healed. For the preservation of the Shire he has sacrificed himself,
even in health, and has no heart to enjoy it. Sam has to choose

First copy of the King's letter

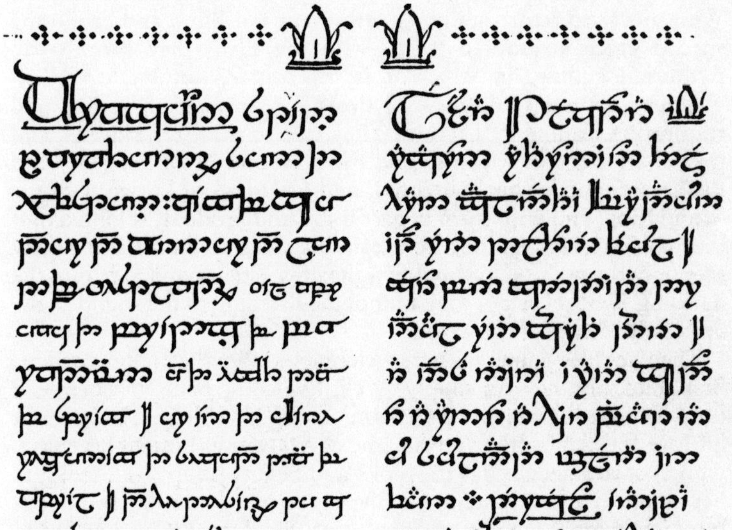

Third copy of the King's letter

between love of master and of wife. In the end he goes with Frodo on a last journey. At night in the woods, where Sam first met Elves on the outward journey, they meet the twilit cavalcade from Rivendell. The Elves and the Three Rings, and Gandalf (Guardian of the Third Age) are going to the Grey Havens, to set sail for the West, never to return. Bilbo is with them. To Bilbo and Frodo the special grace is granted to go with the Elves they loved – an Arthurian ending, in which it is, of course, not made explicit whether this is an 'allegory' of death, or a mode of healing and restoration leading to a return. They ride to the Grey Havens, and take ship: Gandalf with the Red Ring, Elrond (with the Blue) and the greater part of his household, and Galadriel of Lórien with the White Ring, and with them depart Bilbo and Frodo. It is hinted that they come to Eressëa. But Sam standing stricken on the stone quay sees only the white ship slip down the grey estuary and fade into the darkling West. He stays long unmoving listening to the sound of the Sea on the shores of the world.

Then he rides home; his wife welcomes him to the firelight and his first child, and he says simply 'Well, I've come back.'[22] There is a brief epilogue in which we see Sam among his children, a glance at his love for Elanor (the Elvish name of a flower in Lórien) his eldest, who by a strange gift has the looks and beauty of an elven-maid; in her all his love and longing for Elves is resolved and satisfied. He is busy, contented, many times mayor of the Shire, and struggling to finish off the Red Book, begun by Bilbo and nearly completed by Frodo, in which all the events (told in The Hobbit and The Lord [of the Rings]) are recorded. The whole ends with Sam and his wife standing outside Bag-end, as the children are asleep, looking at the stars in the cool spring sky. Sam tells his wife of his bliss and content, and goes in, but as he closes the door he hears the sighing of the Sea on the shores of the world.

It is clear from the words 'we see Sam among his children' that my father was referring to the first version of the Epilogue.

He was persuaded by others to omit the Epilogue from The Lord of the Rings. In a letter to Naomi Mitchison of 25 April 1954 (Letters no. 144) he wrote:

Hobbit-children were delightful, but I am afraid that the only glimpses of them in this book are found at the beginning of vol. I. An epilogue giving a further glimpse (though of a rather exceptional family) has been so universally condemned that I shall not insert it. One must stop somewhere.

He seems both to have accepted and to have regretted that decision. On 24 October 1955, a few days after the publication of The Return of the King, he wrote to Katherine Farrer (Letters no. 173):

I still feel the picture incomplete without something on Samwise and Elanor, but I could not devise anything that would not have destroyed the ending, more than the hints (possibly sufficient) in the appendices.

NOTES

1   The 'Epilogue' text begins at the head of a page, but this is merely because the words ' "Well, I'm back," he said' stand at the foot of the preceding one.

2   '1436' was pencilled in subsequently. Apparently my father first wrote 'And one evening Master Samwise ...', but changed this at once to 'And one evening in March Master Samwise ...' This does not suggest the passage of many years since the sailing of the ship from Mithlond, but that such was the case is immediately plain in the same opening sentence ('and the children were all gathered about him'); the absence of a date in the text as first written must therefore be casual and without significance.

3   *Keleborn:* immediately above the name was spelt *Celeborn*; here, the *K* was changed from *C* in the act of writing the letter.

4   On the development of the legends of Galadriel and Celeborn see *The History of Galadriel and Celeborn* in *Unfinished Tales*, Part Two §IV.

5   *March 18th [> 25th]:* the King had declared in his letter that he would be coming to the Brandywine Bridge on March 25; Elanor had said that that was 'a week today'; and as my father wrote this concluding passage Sam said to Rose at the door of Bag End 'March 18th'. On the change to the 25th, apparently made immediately, see note 7.

6   The brackets are in the original.

7   The change in the King's letter from March 25 to April 2 was in fact, and at first sight very oddly, an emendation made on the B text. This question of the dates is minor, complicated, and explicable. When my father wrote the text A the great day of the King's coming north to the Brandywine Bridge was to be the 25th of March, the date of the destruction of the Ring and the downfall of Sauron (see pp. 59–60); and Elanor said (p. 118) that that was 'a week today', so that the occasion of Sam's conversation with his children recorded in the Epilogue was March 18. When Sam and Rose stood outside Bag End that night Sam said: 'March 18th. Seventeen years ago ...' (p. 118). My father changed '18' to '25' on the manuscript A (and probably at the same time added in the words '*This time* (seventeen years ago)') because he decided, just at that point, that the end of *The Lord of the Rings* (in its Epilogue) should fall on that date (possibly also because he recalled that it was Elanor's birthday, which had of

course been chosen for the same reason); but he failed to postpone the date in the King's letter earlier in A (p. 117).

Writing out the fair copy B, in which he followed A very closely, he momentarily forgot this decision, and repeated the date in A of the King's coming to the Bridge, March 25. Subsequently, while writing B, he realised that this was now erroneous, and changed it to April 2; so at the end of B Sam says (as he had in A): 'March the twenty-fifth! This time seventeen years ago ...'

Elanor's answer to Pippin's question 'When is the second of April?' was changed subsequently on B from 'a week today' to 'a week tomorrow', which is the reading in the typescript C. This, however, was erroneous, since it gives March thirty-one days; 'a week today' was restored in the second version of the Epilogue, p. 127.

8 Chapter-number 'LVIII': the basis of the revised numbering of the chapters of Book Six is not clear to me. The sequence ran from LII 'The Tower of Kirith Ungol' (p. 25) to LX 'The Grey Havens' (p. 110), but on some of the chapters these numbers were reduced by two; here the reduction is by three.

9 Elanor's birth on 25 March (1421) was mentioned in the original draft of 'The Grey Havens', p. 109.

10 In this second version Sam is making notes, which are cited and which are an essential part of the Epilogue, for the filling of the empty pages at the end of the Red Book; and it seems odd that the title 'The End of the Book', so suitable to the second version, should have been used, and rejected, on texts B and C of the first (pp. 119–20).

11 This emendation was made on the typescript only. In 'The Longfather-tree of Master Samwise' in Appendix C Daisy Gamgee was born in 1433 and Primrose in 1435; Bilbo Gamgee was born in the year of the Epilogue, 1436, and was followed by three further children, making thirteen in all.

12 A footnote to the record of the birth of Elanor in *The Tale of Years* states: 'She became known as "the Fair" because of her beauty; many said that she looked more like an elf-maid than a hobbit. She had golden hair, which had been very rare in the Shire; but two others of Samwise's daughters were also golden-haired, and so were many of the children born at this time.' Cf. the reference in 'The Grey Havens' to the golden-haired children born in the Shire in the year 1420 (RK p. 303; see p. 112, note 1).

13 *Sam-dad*: this address to Sam by his children entered in text B of the first version.

14 In the manuscript 'said Sam' is followed by 'sucking his penholder'; this was probably omitted inadvertently, as were other phrases afterwards picked up and reinserted in the typescript.

15 Sam was no doubt thinking of the end of Gimli's song in Moria, by which he was greatly struck (FR p. 330):

> There lies his crown in water deep,
> Till Durin wakes again from sleep.

Or else of Gimli's words when Frodo and Sam looked with him into Mirrormere: 'O Kheled-zâram fair and wonderful! There lies the crown of Durin till he wakes.' ' "What did you see?" said Pippin to Sam, but Sam was too deep in thought to answer' (FR p. 348).

16 Elanor's words refer to RK p. 260 ('Many Partings'): 'But Celeborn said: "Kinsman, farewell! May your doom be other than mine, and your treasure remain with you to the end!" ' For the original form of Celeborn's farewell to Aragorn see p. 64.

17 I do not know of any other reference to this northern journey of Aragorn in the early years of his reign.

18 In the manuscript (which had *ai* forms, later emended, in the names *Iorhail, Perhail, Panthail*) Elanor calls her father *Panthail-adar*.

19 *only a week today:* see note 7, at end.

20 My father's transliteration has *ar ennas i aran Gondor ar Arnor ar Hîr iMbair Annui aníra ...*

21 61 = 16, i.e. year 16 of the Fourth Age, which means that the Fourth Age began in 1421 (see Appendix D to *The Lord of the Rings*, at end).

22 In all the texts of 'The Grey Havens' from the earliest draft Sam said to Rose when he returned to Bag End 'Well, I'm back.' 'Well, I've come back' does not mean the same thing.

APPENDIX

Drawings of Orthanc and Dunharrow

When I wrote Volume VIII, *The War of the Ring*, it entirely and most regrettably escaped my memory that there are several unpublished drawings of Orthanc and Dunharrow in the Bodleian Library. As these are of much interest I reproduce them belatedly here, as a final appendix to the history of *The Lord of the Rings*.

The upper drawing on the page called here 'Orthanc I' shows a conception essentially similar to that of the little sketch 'Orthanc 3' reproduced in VIII.33 and described in the first manuscript of the chapter 'The Voice of Saruman', VIII.61. In this, the tower was founded on a huge arch spanning the great cleft in the rock; flights of stairs led up on two sides to a narrow platform beneath the arch, whence further stairs ran up 'to dark doors on either side, opening in the shadow of the arch's feet'. But in the present drawing the rock of Orthanc is enormously much greater in relation to the tower than in 'Orthanc 3'; the tower has only three tiers (seven in 'Orthanc 3' and in the description associated with it, VIII.32–3); and the horns at the summit are very much smaller.

In the lower drawing on this page, showing the Circle of Isengard in Nan Gurunír between the mountains' arms, is seen the feature described in the original drafting of the chapter 'The Road to Isengard' but rejected from the first completed manuscript (VIII.43, note 23): the western side of the Circle was formed by the mountain-wall itself. The dark letter C was a change made later to the faintly pencilled name of the Wizard's Vale, *Nan Gurunír* becoming *Nan Curunír*.

The page 'Orthanc II' carries two designs for 'Orthanc's roof'; and on 'Orthanc III' the final conception is seen emerging, in which the 'rock' of Orthanc becomes itself the 'tower'. The drawing on the right has in fact been previously published: it was used in *The Lord of the Rings Calendar 1977*, and so appears in *Pictures by J. R. R. Tolkien*, no. 27 (see VIII.44, note 26).

The two pages of drawings of Dunharrow are not easy to interpret, more especially 'Dunharrow I' (for the early conceptions of Dunharrow and the first sketches see VIII.235 ff.). Of 'Dunharrow I' it can at least be said that this idea of the approach to the Hold was never described in words. Apparently, the path winding up from the valley passed near the top of the cliff through the great door in the foreground and entered a steeply ascending tunnel, climbing up by stairs inside the cliff, the head of which can be seen emerging from a large opening or hole in the flat land above. The single menhir, first mentioned in the text F of the original work on the chapter 'The Muster of Rohan' (VIII.246) as standing in the rock-ringed floor of the Hold, is seen; but since there is no sign of the lines of standing stones across the upland (nor of the Púkel-men at the turns in the climbing path) I would be inclined to place this drawing after the earliest drafts of the chapter and the little sketches reproduced in VIII.239 but before the writing of the text F.

A very puzzling feature of this drawing is the wavy line at bottom left, hiding one of the bends in the climbing path.

The upper drawing on the page 'Dunharrow II' has a general likeness in the lie of the mountain side to the coloured drawing reproduced as the first frontispiece (but which should have been the second) to *The War of the Ring*, but there the resemblance ceases. In that other picture a double line of huge standing stones crosses the upland from the brink of the cliff to a dark cleft in the mountain, where the road so marked out disappears; and I suggested (VIII.250) that the dark cleft is ' "the gate of the Hold", the "Hold" itself, the "recess" or "amphitheatre" with doors and windows in the cliff at the rear, being in this picture invisible.' In the present drawing the Púkel-men are seen at the turns of the path coming up from the valley; at the top of the cliff the road continues to wind, but the turns are now marked by pointed stones. There is then a straight stretch across the upland field, unmarked by stones; and the road passing (apparently) between two stones or pillars leads into the Hold, in which the door into the cliff behind can be seen. In the left-hand lower drawing the Púkel-men reappear, and in the right-hand drawing a double line of cone-shaped stones leads across the upland and into the Hold, with a single stone standing in the middle of the 'amphitheatre'.

My guess is that the upper drawing on this page shows a stage in the development of the conception of Dunharrow when the Púkel-men had emerged, but not the double line of stones: these are seen at the moment of their emergence in one of the lower sketches. In relation to the manuscript evidence, 'Dunharrow I' would then belong with, but actually precede, the text F of 'The Muster of Rohan', in which both the Púkel-men (then called the Hoker-men) and the lines of stones are present.

Orthanc I

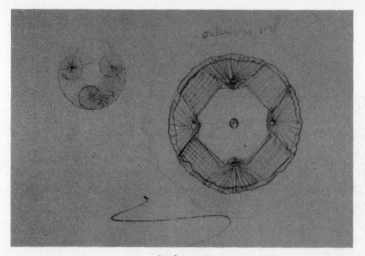

Orthanc II

Orthanc III

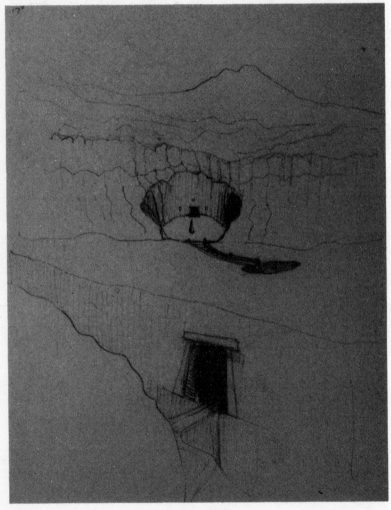

Dunharrow I

Dunharrow II

INDEX

This index is made with the same degree of fulness as those to the previous volumes dealing with the history of the writing of *The Lord of the Rings*. As before, names are mostly given in a 'standard' form; and certain names are not indexed: those occurring in the titles of chapters etc.; those of the recipients of letters; and those appearing in the reproductions of manuscript pages. The word *passim* is again used to mean that in a long run of references there is a page here and there where the name does not occur.

elanor Golden flower of Lórien. (114–15), 124, 132. For Sam's daughter *Elanor* see under *Gamgee*.

Elbereth Varda. 112

Eldamar Elvenhome, the region of Aman in which the Elves dwelt. 58

Elder Days 68

Elendil 56, 58–9; *the Horn of Elendil (Windbeam)* 4

Elessar (The) Elfstone, Aragorn. 52, 58, 117, 119, 128. See *Aragorn*.

Elf-friends 92; *Elf-maid* 134, *Elf-prince* 92

Elfhelm the Marshal Rider of Rohan. 59

Elfstone, (The) Aragorn. 64, 66–7, 117, 119, 128; the green stone 56; Sindarin *Edhelharn* 128–9. See *Elessar*.

Elladan Son of Elrond. 57, 66, 127

Ellonel Transient name preceding Arwen. 66. See *Finduilas* (1).

Elrohir Son of Elrond. 57, 66, 127

Elrond 25, 33, 52–3, 58–9, 63–4, 66–7, 69, 109, 111, 115, 119, 124–5, 132; *Council of Elrond* 71. Sons of Elrond 57, (63); see *Elladan, Elrohir*.

Elven- *Elven-cloak* 14, 29, 48, 50 (and see *Lórien*); -*grace* 122; -*light* 125; -*lord* 49; -*maid* 132

Elves 7, 9, 14, 26, 52–3, 58, 89, 109, 111, 115–16, 119, 123–5, 127, 132

Elvish (with reference to language) 58, 72, 117–18, 121, 126, 132; Elvish cited 30, 46–7, 51, 56–7, 62, 64, 68, 70, 72–3, 112, 128–9; (with other reference) 8, 26, 34, 69, 116, 125

Emmeril Original name of the wife of Denethor. 54. See *Finduilas* (2).

Emrahil Transient name preceding *Arwen*. 66. See *Finduilas* (1).

Emyn Muil 7

Encircling Mountains (about the plain of Gondolin) 44. See *Gochressiel, (Mountains of) Turgon*.

Ents 7, 9, 53, 63, 71, 116, 119, 123; *Entwives* 63, 116, 120, 123; *Entings* 71

Éomer, King Éomer 7, 48, 52, 54–5, 57, 61–3, 66–8, 73, 123

Eorl the Young 68, 72

Éowyn 52, 54–5, 57, 59, 62–3, 68, 123; *Lady of Rohan* 62

Ephel Dúath 22, 32, 35

Erebor The Lonely Mountain. 119

Erech, Stone of Erech 15–17; the *palantír* of Erech 15

Ered Lithui The Ash Mountains. 11, 32, 35; *the north(ern) range* 33, 39

Ered Nimrais 16. See *White Mountains*.

Eressëa See *Tol Eressëa*.

Erien Replaced, and replaced by, *Arien*. 120–1. See *Arien, Eirien*.

Ethir Anduin 15–16; the *Ethir* 15

Etymologies In Vol.V, *The Lost Road*. 73

Gorbag   Orc of Minas Morgul (but also of the Tower of Kirith Ungol, see 9). 8–10, 13–14, 18, 23–4, 26, 28

Gorgor   8 (*fields of Gorgor, the Gorgor plain*), 22 (*valley of Gorgor*); replaced by *Gorgoroth*. See *Kirith Gorgor*.

Gorgoroth   20, 23, 34, 51. See *Gorgor, Kirith Gorgor*.

Gorgos   Eastern guard-tower of Kirith Ungol as the main pass into Mordor. 28

Gram, Mount   119. See *Golfimbul*.

Great River   49; *the River* 116. See *Anduin*.

Great Sea   See *(The) Sea*.

Green Dragon   The inn at Bywater. 82

Greenfields, Battle of   101, 107; ~ *of the Green Fields* 119

Green Hills   In the Shire. 99–100, 107

Greenway   83

Greenwood the Great   Later name of Mirkwood. 123

Greyflood, River   72, 76, 103

Grey Havens   53, 80, 109, 112, 132; *the Havens* 52–3, 112, 115, 125. See *Mithlond*.

Grey Wood   (also *Greywood, Grey Woods*). Under *Amon Dîn*. 61, 67, 70

Gríma   Wormtongue. 65, 73. (Replaced *Frána*.)

Gwaewar   See *Gwaihir*.

Gwaihir   'The Windlord', Eagle of the North; earlier name *Gwaewar* (45). (1) In the Elder Days, vassal of Thorondor. 45. (2) In the Third Age, descendant of Thorondor. 7, 44–5

Gwirith   April. 129

Half-elven   See *Finduilas* (1).

Halflings   46–7. See *Periain, Periannath*.

Háma   Eleventh King of the Mark. 68. (Replaced by *Brytta*, also named *Léofa*.)

Harad   The South. *Men of Harad* 15

Haradwaith   People of the South. 15–17; *Haradrians* 17

Harrowdale   123

Hasufel   Aragorn's horse of Rohan. 61 (error for *Arod*), 70, 72

Havens, The   See *Grey Havens*.

Hayward, Hob   Hobbit; a guard at the Brandywine Bridge. 79–80

Helm   Ninth King of the Mark. 72

Helm's Deep   63

Henneth Annûn   50, 55

High Elves   124

Hobbiton   80, 82–3, 85, 87–8, 99–101, 103, 105–7, 118, 127; *the Hill of Hobbiton* 103; *the Old Mill* 88, 106, *the Old Grange* (88), 106, *the bridge* 89

Hobbit, The   12, 119, 132

Holbytlan   (Old English) Hobbits. 47

Voronwë Elf of Gondolin. 44
Vultures Steeds of the Winged Nazgûl. 3–4

War of the Ring 111; *the War* 100
Watchers, The At the gate of the Tower of Kirith Ungol. 23, 25–6
Waymoot Village in the Westfarthing where the roads from Sarn Ford and Little Delving joined the East Road. 92, 100, 106; *Waymeet* 106
Weathertop 6, 75–6, 78, 109, 112
West, The 67, 83, 132; *island of the West* 53; *King of the West* 74; *the True West* 110. See *Captains of, Men of, the West.*
Westernesse Númenor. 49
Westlands 117, 128. See *Aragorn.*
Westmarch See *Red Book of Westmarch.*
Westron 30
White army 8
White Crown 55–6; on Aragorn's standard 15, 56
White Downs 92–3, 109
White Mountains 119, 122; *the mountains* 15, 116; *the Dales* 15. See *Ered Nimrais.*
White Ship The ship that bore the Ringbearers from the Grey Havens. 120, 123, 132; other references to the ship 109–10, 133
White Tower See *Minas Tirith.*
White Tree of Númenor Nimloth. 58. (The sapling found on Mount Mindolluin 57–8.)
Whitfoot, Will Mayor of the Shire. 81, 108, 110; called *Flourdumpling* 81
Whitfurrows Village in the Eastfarthing (replaced *Bamfurlong*). 107
Wild Men, Wild Man (of Druadan Forest) 22, 61, 68; *Wild Men of the Woods* 57; *Ghân of the Wild Woods* 56, 67
Windbeam The horn of Elendil. 4
Wise, The 111
Wizards (not referring expressly to Gandalf or Saruman) 26, 77. *The Wizard King* 6–7; *the Wizard's Vale* 136 (see *Nan Gurunír*).
Wold (of Rohan) 63, 71
Woody End 52, 101, 109, 112
Wormtongue 64–5, 73, 100. See *Frána, Gríma.*

Yagûl Orc of Minas Morghul. 13. (Replaced by *Gorbag.*)
Yavanna 58
Yoreth See *Ioreth.*
Younger Days 68

Zirakzigil One of the Mountains of Moria (Silvertine). 45. Earlier name *Zirakinbar* 45